OPAITU

THE CALLING

ANNE COWELL

First edition, 2017

Paperback ISBN 978-0-473-40421-5

Published by:
Anesco Limited
PO Box 89204, Torbay, Auckland, New Zealand, 0742

www.annecowell.com

For my children, Scott and Sheri

Thank you for all the love and joy you have given me through the years, and for making me so proud of you both as you have grown into beautiful, caring adults.

ACKNOWLEDGEMENTS

I would like to especially thank my husband, Bill, for his quiet acceptance and support. I know he raises his eyebrows, thinking, "Here she goes again," each time I rush off on another tangent, following a newfound passion. But he has the good sense to let me go ahead and enjoy the process that each new challenge offers me.

Thanks to my friends and family who are always there for me, giving me love and acceptance, which I believe are so important to each and every one of us to develop to our full potential and to live meaningful lives. I wouldn't have been brave enough to go through with this without each of you being there for me in your own special way. I am so lucky to be surrounded by so much love and support.

A huge thank you to my copy editor, Anne Slight, for her incredible talent and advice, for bringing her knowledge of the written word to bear, and for her honesty and integrity throughout this journey. Also for her diplomatic and gentle way of suggesting when something wasn't quite right!

Thank you to all my readers for your support, which is appreciated more than you could know.

Rika

CHAPTER ONE

With a band of tom-tom drums playing raucously in her chest and a feeling of impending doom, Rika bowed, placing both hands into Levi's glimmering gold palms. She had only ever been in his presence once before, when she had first arrived in Opaitu. Why had she been summoned now? She didn't want to go back to Earth.

As her hands connected with the light radiating from his bright golden body, a sense of calm flowed over Rika. The drums stopped bashing her heart to shreds and the dread that had enveloped her just a moment ago disappeared. Rika's amber eyes locked onto Levi's all-knowing blue eyes. She smiled bravely.

"Hello Rika, please follow me," Levi said in a deep, soothing voice as he glided away. She hurried after him through a golden archway into a room sparkling with colour. Rika remembered this gorgeous place. It signified her introduction to this magical world.

Gwen stood at the far end of the chamber. Her ethereal beauty once again amazed Rika. Gwen's light enveloped Rika in waves of goodness and understanding.

"Rika, welcome back. You are looking fabulous," Gwen said as Rika placed her hands in Gwen's outstretched palms in ritualistic greeting. Gwen motioned for Rika to sit on a sofa with her.

Rika smiled and sat. Her vocal chords had taken flight. What was wrong with her? She wasn't often speechless. But she recollected being like this when she first met these unearthly beings. Their presence was overwhelming.

Levi smiled and sat down in an armchair facing Rika and Gwen. "You will be wondering why we have requested this meeting, Rika. Do not be concerned that you have made any mistakes. You have been a very law-abiding citizen." He chuckled at Rika's surprised look.

"You read my mind," Rika managed to say.

Levi nodded and continued: "Although humans on Earth have progressed technologically, medically and in other practical ways, there is still much that is wrong. Not only does this cause pain and suffering to mankind, but also to animals, plants and the very planet that humans rely on for their survival. The behaviour of many people is as unrefined and barbaric as it was centuries ago. By now the human race on Earth was expected to have evolved to a much higher spiritual level, based on love and kindness. But negative emotions of hate, fear and greed, and the yearning for power over others, are preventing many from ascending to a higher dimension. And as a result, other life forms on the planet are being destroyed. The world cannot support the abuse and disregard much longer."

Rika listened to Levi's words with a heavy heart for the destiny of her people and Earth and its creatures, but she couldn't understand why he was telling her about it. What could it possibly have to do with her?

Levi continued as though hearing Rika's thoughts. "You have come to our attention as a candidate to assist in a crucial mission. The Universe has decided to send help to Earth, but of course, we may not interfere with man's free will, as it is a cardinal law of the Universe."

Rika's jaw dropped open, as she realised with alarm why she was summoned.

"Yes, Rika, we require you to return to Earth."

Rika felt the colour drain from her face. "No!" she blurted.

She was immediately ashamed of her outburst and rudeness. "I'm sorry, I didn't mean to be discourteous. But I thought that I would never have to go back to Earth. My last experience there was too hard." Rika shuddered.

"We understand that Rika, and would not expect you to have another life like that. You conquered adversity and rose above your suffering to be a decent and beautiful human being, worthy of the next phase of your existence. We do not expect you to go through anything like that again. In fact, quite the opposite. Should you agree to this mission, you may ascend to the next realm without having to complete all your life-lessons here in Opaitu. Of course, as with all things human, you have free will. You may decline the mission."

Rika's head was spinning. This plea was huge. She took a few moments to gather her thoughts. "I don't know how to respond. I feel honoured that you have chosen me, but I don't feel worthy of your selection. And I have no wish to fast-track by skipping any lessons in Opaitu. I love it here," she said truthfully.

Levi laughed. "It will be your choice when the time comes, whether to continue your life here or to fast-track, as you call it. It is also only fair that we supply more information before expecting your decision. We shall be meeting with a few hundred other candidates tomorrow morning to brief you all."

Rika replied, "Thank you. I will keep an open mind and learn more tomorrow."

Gwen stood. "We appreciate your willingness to hear what we have planned. And as Levi said, it will be up to you whether you wish to become involved. We will meet in the Ruby Room at dawn."

Rika stood and bowed to the Tuerians, then turned and found her way out of the room in a semi-trance.

As she walked outside into the golden light of the afternoon, the calm she had felt when near the Tuerians deserted her. She wriggled into her SkyPod cockpit and huddled over in despair. Feelings of dread engulfed her as hot tears dripped onto her lap. She had thought she would never shed another tear. Her mind raced back, unbidden, to her last couple of years on Earth.

CHAPTER TWO

Rika shivered as earthly emotions returned in full force. Her body broke into a cold sweat as she remembered things that hadn't touched her since she had arrived in Opaitu. She was now re-living that fateful time, scene by scene, with all the emotions, guilt and pain tearing at her.

Back in 1872, Mother was battling to feed and clothe her children since their father had died in the collapse at the coal mine. Things were tough for Mother until she met Austin in the spring of 1873. He had been charming and full of love for Mother. They were married within just a few months. Austin moved the family to the country and life was good. He went to work at a nearby farm and Mother taught the children to sew and cook and how to grow vegetables. Rika loved the smell of the soil and the feel of her hands in the damp earth. She took special care in tending to the vegetables, and she and her little brother, Colin, enjoyed watching their plants grow. Their days were full of joy and laughter as they looked after their garden and played hide and seek in the woods at the back of their little cottage.

Austin didn't pay much attention to the children, but he wasn't unkind to them and they were happy because their mother was happy. But the children never saw anyone else, and they were forbidden to leave the property. They had only each other. The isolation sometimes made Rika sad as she longed for the company of other young girls. But at least she had Colin and her mother, and her mother had a man to look after her again.

But sadly the happiness was short-lived. About a year after her mother and Austin married, things began to change. Her stepfather started distilling alcohol. At first he would drink only a small glass each day. Within just a few weeks, Rika noticed how he began drinking more and more. His temperament changed when he was drunk and he became angry with all of them for no reason. One day he hit Colin, knocking him over. Rika's mother ran to her son, hugging him to her protectively. She yelled at Austin to leave the boy alone. The drunken man was beyond reason and struck out at her too.

From that point on their lives changed for the worse as their stepfather became abusive to all of them, and Colin and Rika began to fear him. Mother became timid and sickly and spent more and more time in her bed.

Monster, as they now referred to their stepfather, told them that their mother was ill and needed to rest. They should leave her alone. He brewed up some foul-smelling concoction which he gave to her twice a day. Rika was sure it was making her mother worse, not helping her to get better. One morning, when her stepfather was still sober, Rika suggested to him that he stop giving her the potion he was making, and rather let Rika look after her mother by feeding her soups and herbs made from her garden vegetables. Monster became angry at Rika's suggestion and forbade Rika to interfere.

Their mother seemed to lose her zest for life and Rika watched in horror as she changed, within just a few months, from a beautiful, lively woman of grace and charm, into a wasted old lady who didn't even seem to know her own children.

Whenever Monster went out to work, Rika would force some soup into her mother, bathe her with water warmed over the fire and try to make her comfortable. But she didn't respond to Rika's care. It was as though Mother's mind had left her failing body. She seldom even spoke.

As Mother faded into oblivion, Monster became angrier and more violent. He blamed Rika for her mother's illness and began to lash out at her and Colin. Most evenings he would became 'sleep-drunk' as Colin called it, and he would eventually pass out.

One morning, while Rika was tending to the vegetable garden, she heard a high-pitched scream. She dropped her spade and ran into the cottage to find Colin standing wide-eyed and shaking, beside his mother's bed. Mother's body was heaving with convulsions, her breath shallow and rasping. Rika took her mother's hands in hers and whispered, "Mother, we are here."

Mother's eyes sprang open as Rika spoke, then her body relaxed and she smiled. Rika pulled Colin towards their mother and motioned for him to cuddle her. His tears dripped onto her face as he put his little arms around her. She spoke for the first time in months, though her voice was just a croak: "My babies, I love you. I am so sorry." She took a long shuddering breath and then became totally still. Rika gasped as she sensed that her Mother had left them forever. She pulled Colin into her arms and hugged him tight.

"Colin, Mother's gone to another place now where she will not suffer any more. Say goodbye to her."

Colin took a last glance at his mother and ran, screaming, from the room. Rika laid her mother's hands over her chest and gently closed her eyelids. She bent over her mother's inert form and gave her a soft kiss on her forehead. Rika felt a strange sense of tranquillity wash over her. She pulled the sheet over her mother's head, then turned and calmly walked out of the room.

Rika tried to blank out the visions. She didn't want to re-live what followed. But she'd opened the floodgates now, and the memories poured out.

Rika realised that she had known deep-down that her mother wasn't going to get better, but the reality of her death was such a shock. The calmness she had felt as she said her last goodbye to Mother was now replaced with dread.

What was going to happen to Colin and her now? Could she get Colin away from here? She had no money to support them and no-one to turn to. At least here she could feed them using her herbs and vegetables. After much wrestling with her logic and emotions, Rika decided that they had no choice but to remain here with their stepfather.

But nothing could have prepared Rika for what she discovered some days later on waking up. Colin was gone! He wasn't in his bed and he didn't respond when she called. A jolt of dread hit her stomach. She ran outside shouting his name as loud as she could. She searched for him all day, calling for him until her voice was just a croak. Nothing!

She finally dragged herself back to the cottage as daylight was fading. Monster was home and already drinking. He gave Rika a sly grin as she burst into the cottage, hoping beyond hope that her little brother was safely inside.

"Where's Colin?" Rika asked in a shaky voice.

"He's gone. You didn't think I wanted him, did you?"

Rika's heart hammered in her chest. "What do you mean, he's gone? What have you done with him?"

"He'll be fine. I took him to the orphanage. They will look after him. Don't you worry that pretty head of yours," he added with a grin.

Rika charged at him, beating her fists against his chest. "How could you do that? He's only a little boy. Go get him back. I will look after him."

"You don't get it, do you?" he asked as he pushed Rika roughly away from him.

"Why would you send my little brother to an orphanage? I looked after him while Mamma was ill and I can continue to do that. Please bring him home."

"No Rika, I won't do that. I want only you here – all to myself." Monster laughed.

It was like a knife in her heart. Mother was dead, and now he had sent Colin away so that she would be alone with him. What was his plan for her? She had no idea, but she knew it wasn't good.

Rika didn't want to remember more. The guilt came flooding back and she sobbed. She didn't want to recall the time that followed or the anguish that had haunted her every day, thinking how different things could have been if she'd been brave enough to take Colin and run away when they had the chance. Even though she still didn't know what had become of Colin, the guilt had been taken away when she arrived in Opaitu. Now it was back, in full force.

Thank goodness, Monster left Rika alone for the rest of that night. She felt terrible. Even when her mother was sick, Rika had been able to deal with her emotions and just get on with doing her best to look after her brother and her mother. But this? Colin being sent away was more than Rika could bear. She collapsed on her bed, wracked with sobs until her exhausted mind and body finally gave in to the oblivion of a deep sleep.

The following morning she jolted awake as Monster drunkenly crashed through the door of her room. He grabbed her arm and dragged her out of her bed. "Get yourself washed and make me some breakfast. Now that there's no Mother or Colin to look after, you can finally give me all your attention. Be a good girl and do as you are told."

CHAPTER THREE

Rika shivered as she remembered that moment. Although she had been young and innocent at that time, she had known deep down that there was more to this than just cooking and cleaning for the man. Unbidden, Rika's mind returned to those days on Earth.

Rika did as she was told. She was numbed with grief, guilt and loss, so she didn't have the strength to consider that there could be another option. She cooked and cleaned and only spoke if Monster required her to. The only time she felt any sense of peace was when she was tending to her garden. The warmth of the sun on her skin, the feel of the soil through her fingers, the singing of the birds in the trees, and the buzzing of the insects gave her some sense of tranquillity and freedom. Colin was on her mind almost constantly. She imagined his laughter as they chased each other across the fields and into the woods. She feared for his safety. By behaving herself, maybe one day Monster would relent and bring him home.

He continued drinking heavily. Often he got violent and would shout at Rika and hit her. But mostly he just slumped into what Colin had referred to as 'sleep-drunk'.

Sometimes, when he wasn't as drunk as usual, he was even affectionate towards her, but there was something in the way he touched Rika then that made her feel uncomfortable. One evening, he suddenly hugged her fiercely and turned her face towards his, kissing her hard on the mouth. She pushed against him and tried to release herself from his strong grasp.

"Relax Rika, I just want to show you how much I love you."

Rika's heart raced. She didn't understand what was happening, and she was so confused. Didn't she want to be loved? She had no-one else to love her, so why was she so frightened. Rika wrestled with her emotions. She so badly wanted to be loved but this didn't seem right.

In a moment of clarity, she knew she had to leave here and get away from this man. And most of all, she had to find Colin. She lay awake all night as she planned her escape.

The next morning when her stepfather went out to work, she dressed as warmly as she could, pulled a blanket off her bed and wrapped it around herself. She took the half loaf of bread that was left on the shelf and ran out of the cottage, without looking back.

Her heart hammered in her chest. She ran towards the woods, eager to get out of sight. Her biggest fear right now was that Monster would suddenly appear. Once she was hidden by the trees, she turned to look back. Everything was calm and quiet. Thank goodness.

As the trees thinned, Rika was able to see what lay ahead of her. The land sloped gently down towards a stream then climbed steeply up towards rocky outcrops. Mountains faded into the distance, their peaks dusted in white. Rika shivered. The temperature had already started to plummet over the last few days and she knew that it would be snowing soon. She looked left and right, but decided to continue to head down to the stream, in the opposite direction to the one that her stepfather took to work every day.

Rika took a deep breath and continued on her way. She found a place to jump across the stream, managing to keep herself dry. She knelt down, filled her hands with the cold water and drank as much as she could. She didn't know when she'd have another chance to drink. She managed to reach the rocky outcrops before nightfall, and found an overhanging rock under which she decided to stay to give her some shelter.

The night was so dark and scary. Rika was colder and more alone than she'd ever been. What had she done? But even as she thought about her warm home, she knew that if she went back her life wouldn't be worth living. As soon as it was light, she'd keep going. She would be warmer when she started moving again and hopefully she'd soon find someone to help her.

Rika woke to a white world. It had snowed during the night and she was now freezing cold and damp. Her teeth chattered. Her stomach growled. Luckily, she had tucked the bread into her blanket with her, so the warmth from her body had stopped it from freezing. She took a small bite and chewed for as long as she could before swallowing. She knew she had to make the bread last so she savoured every mouthful. She dragged up her aching body and started walking. She was stiff and her limbs were so cold that she could hardly move. But she knew she had to keep going.

The snow eased for the first part of the day and Rika managed to find her way down the other side of the rocky hill until she reached a wide valley. Sitting down on a fallen tree trunk, she picked at some bread before continuing to move up the valley. The clouds descended and Rika could barely see in front of her – the world consisted of only swirling white powder. Her *body shook with cold and exhaustion. Her mind was losing focus. She tripped over something, twisting her ankle as she fell. She screamed and tried to get up, but her foot couldn't bear any weight. She shouted for help until her voice was just a whisper. No help arrived. Crying in pain and despair, she pulled herself up, determined to find Colin. She tried to hop on her good leg, but it was impossible in the snow, so she dragged her injured foot until the pain was so bad that she collapsed. At that second, Rika knew she was going to die of exposure, right here in this valley. The pain in her ankle was nothing compared to the guilt she felt at her inability to save her mother and brother. As she lost consciousness her pain and anguish receded.*

Her last awareness was of a warm golden light enveloping her.

Rika's body shook as she clamped her eyes shut, trying to shut out that life on Earth. She pleaded silently, "Please, take the memories away."

She felt the lightest touch of warmth on her face. Her tears were gently wiped away. She opened her eyes to see golden light radiating all around her. Gwen's tender smile swam into Rika's vision, and her painful memories receded into the back of her mind. She inhaled deeply. Tranquillity enveloped her. Rika's body stopped shaking, and her guilt abated.

She was no longer that child, tormented by an abusive man. Since her death there was light. And peace. And overwhelming love.

"Thank you, Gwen," Rika murmured, as the golden light vaporised the memories.

Rika was once again in Opaitu where pain and suffering no longer had a place. The guilt no longer belonged to her. She was a complete and perfect human being with no scars on her soul. She was beautiful. She was a miracle of creation. She was at peace and she was in love with life. Love and warmth surrounded her. She was love. She was warmth. She was a child. She was a teenager. She was twenty. She was thirty. She was two hundred. She was a two-hundred-year-old child. Age was immeasurable here. She was infinite.

CHAPTER FOUR

Rika brought her SkyPod in to land in the pale light just before dawn. The docking station was buzzing with activity, and the stairway leading to the Ruby Room was full of beautiful people. The anticipation in the air was palpable. Rika wasn't sure if she was excited or nervous.

"Hey, Rika!"

Rika turned towards the voice. Max leaned casually against the wall near the entrance to the building. She grinned and ran up the last few stairs to meet him. Rika was always shocked at how fast Max moved. By the time she got to the top step, he was already there. He lifted her off her feet, stepped back a couple of paces away from the stairway and, with her in his arms, he swung her around. Laughter crinkled the corners of his dark brown eyes. He gave her a loud smacking kiss on her cheek and gently put her down.

Rika laughed. "You always give me the best welcome, Max. I don't need to ask how you are. I can see you are fantastic. It's so good to see you here. I need your support. Yesterday I nearly had a heart attack when I realised that I might go back to Earth."

Max chuckled. "Why would you worry? It's just

16

another adventure. Now we know the things we do, there's nothing to be afraid of."

Rika smiled warmly at Max. "You're right, and I love your attitude. I'll be as positive as I can about it. If we do go on this mission, there's nobody I'd rather be with than you."

"Well, let's go and see what's in store for us, shall we?" Max asked as he stepped behind Rika and gently lifted her up once again. He dangled her from his arms like a puppet and then rested her feet on his. They marched as one, stretching their arms out in perfect timing with their footsteps.

"I can walk on my own two feet, you know," Rika giggled as she stepped off his feet and turned around to face Max. He was dazzling. Literally! He was doing that 'thing' of his again. She laughed as coloured lights radiated from his eyes, and he started singing. He had a fantastic voice which sounded like he had a band of instruments playing in the background. His lights danced over Rika's body. Her body tingled as it started moving rhythmically with the song and light, with a will of its own. She shimmered and shimmied like a child playing in the rain. It was liberating and fun.

It was contagious. As Max cast his light around, people leapt and spun and wiggled their way up the staircase. Laughter and joy vibrated through the air. They cartwheeled and flick-flacked until they were out of the path of Max's light.

He turned off the light show and flung himself high into the air and backwards into a double somersault. A deep-throated laugh bubbled out of him. Rika shook her head and giggled like a child enjoying a clown show. No wonder she wanted to be around Max. He brought even more joy to life here. He was such a crazy, free spirit.

Max linked his arm in Rika's as they followed the others into the building and towards the Ruby Room.

Rika gasped in awe as she entered the room. It was

glorious. Light from thousands of rubies flickered, pulsing to the beat of faraway drums.

Rika and Max found seats together and sat down. Once everyone had settled, the music softened.

The room went dark and words 'Opaitu – The Calling' shone around the chamber.

The words faded and Earth appeared as though they were looking down onto the beautiful planet from space.

Angelic voices harmonised as orchestral music ebbed and flowed around them. Rika couldn't make out any specific words. Shivers ran down her spine as one voice rose above the others. It was a haunting sound, a sort of wailing chant, and sounds of creaking and groaning vibrated through the back of Rika's chair. There was a deafening bang. Enormous clouds of smoke rose from the planet. A mighty tearing, wrenching sound filled their ears as a vast chasm broke across Earth, tearing down from Europe and slicing through Africa. A tsunami raced across the Atlantic Ocean, wiping out Brazil in an instant, along with other parts of South America. Earth shook. Volcanoes blew their tops along the Pacific Ring of Fire. The San Andreas fault split open.

The music built to a crescendo. Earth exploded.

It had all happened within seconds.

The vision disappeared. The room was deathly silent. Darkness enveloped them.

Levi's sad tones broke the spell. "Goodbye Earth."

Rika's heart raced. Were they too late? Had man annihilated Earth? Max grabbed Rika's hand and squeezed.

Gwen said, "That is what we want to prevent."

There was a collective sigh around the room as everyone realised it had just been a show to get their attention.

Soft light enveloped them as muted sparkles from the rubies glistened sporadically.

Levi continued in a sombre voice. "Since we spoke to you all yesterday, each of you will have re-visited some of your time on Earth. We apologise for bringing those memories back into focus and causing you pain. We did that to re-connect you to your life there and remind you of the hardships people on Earth still face. The problems have changed over time, but pain and suffering are still as prevalent these days, if not even more so. As man's technology and intellect has increased, so has his lust and greed for power. Only now he is capable of destroying everything. Not only capable, but some even have the desire to obliterate all."

Gwen took over. "There are those who, in the name of some cause or belief, are prepared to take lives, sometimes even their own. And they have no concern for the very planet that plays host to them and supplies them with their every need. It seems inconceivable, but this is escalating exponentially as technology advances. So, the Universe is calling Opaitu to assist. We may not interfere with man's free will, or show ourselves directly to man on Earth, but we have come up with some ideas."

The Tuerians went into explanations and basic concepts, highlighting what could and couldn't be done, what was and wasn't allowed. They encouraged discussion with the candidates. Once everyone was clear about the mission, what it meant to each of them individually and as a team, the expected outcome, what obstacles may stand in their way and how important this mission was for Earth and the human race, they were given time to think carefully about their decisions.

"I'm in," said Max. "Things sound pretty bad there. They need as much help as they can get. Come on, Rika. Join in. We may even have some fun while we save Earth."

"I'll do it, Max. I want to help. It's not right that so many people suffer. And our role there sounds quite different to my last experience on Earth. And as you pointed out before, now that we know life here, there's nothing to be afraid of. Please make sure you aren't too far away from me though. I may need your craziness."

Once everyone had made their decision, Levi said, "Thank you all for your consideration and especially to those of you who have decided to help Earth. You will be returning there during the second decade of their twenty-first century. The timing when each of you begins your journey on Earth will be slightly staggered in Earth-time. However, we will all travel to the Milky Way Galaxy and Earth together. We leave tomorrow. We shall supply everything you need for the journey. Please meet here at sunrise tomorrow. Thank you for your love and compassion."

Robyn

CHAPTER FIVE

Robyn stepped off the school bus trying not to stumble. With head down she told herself, "Don't cry, don't cry." She could sense four pairs of eyes maliciously boring into her back.

When the bus was out of sight, Robyn picked up the pace and rushed home. As she neared her driveway, she heard a familiar yap. At the other side of the gate Paprika spun in circles in her excitement and her whole body wagged in delight. The dog gave a big yawn and it was as though she said hello as she voiced the familiar sound, 'Oawro'.

"Paprika, I missed you," Robyn said as she opened the gate. Robyn sat on the deck to cuddle her dog. Her bubble of restraint burst. Tears flooded down her face. Paprika, sensing her despair, nuzzled into Robyn, licking her neck, and then settled down with her head in Robyn's lap.

"Oh Paprika, I'm so happy that you love me. It's been another terrible day. Thank goodness Hayley's back from holiday tomorrow. It's been awful without her around. At least I have you." Robyn wiped her eyes with the back of her hand.

Paprika looked up into Robyn's eyes. There was something so understanding about Paprika's gorgeous amber eyes. It was as though she knew so much more than a dog should. "You're just the best dog in the world. Come on. I'll be okay now I'm home with you. Let's play. Where's your ball?"

Paprika shot off to retrieve the deflated, chewed, old soccer ball she loved so much. "Where's the other one?" Robyn asked. With a short playful woof, the border collie turned and ran to the back of the house, encouraging Robyn to follow her. As Robyn rounded the corner, Paprika poised with the beaten-up old soccer ball in her mouth and her gaze focused on a basketball lying near her feet. Robyn picked up the basketball and the dog ran away a few paces, then turned back to look at Robyn, waiting for the throw. As the basketball bounced, Paprika thumped it with both front paws. The other ball was still gripped in her mouth as she knocked the basketball back to Robyn. "Good goalie, good girl! Again?"

"Hi, Robyn," called Carol through the open kitchen window. "Paprika has been waiting for you at the gate for about ten minutes. It's uncanny the way she seems to know when you're due home. Brad texted to ask me to fetch him from gymnastics at four, so I'm leaving soon. I thought that as it's such a beautiful day, we should go to the beach for a swim. I know Paprika will be keen."

"Good idea Mum. I'll get into my togs. Come Pappi." Within a few minutes they were in the car, Paprika in the back of the station wagon. Paprika spotted Brad as they neared the school gates. Her tail thumped against the window in excitement.

"Hi, I see you've brought my togs, so I guess we're going to the beach. Hi, Paprika," Brad said as he climbed into the back seat. Paprika put her front paws on the back of the seat and licked Brad's neck and face. She made funny little whimpering sounds in her enthusiasm.

They arrived at the beach in less than five minutes. Paprika had started barking as soon as she realised where they were going. Robyn picked up the ball and thrower, grabbed a towel off the back seat and hopped out. "Paprika, sit... wait." Robyn commanded as she opened the rear door of the car. Paprika sat trembling with excitement as Robyn clipped the lead onto her collar.

"Okay, let's go. Don't pull, Paprika. Mum, I'll meet you guys down on the beach." When they reached the sand, Robyn told Paprika to sit and wait, unclipped her lead and at the word 'Go!' the dog charged across the damp sand at breakneck speed. She stopped several metres away and waited for the first throw of the ball. As it bounced she leapt up, snatching it from the air in one fluid movement. Before her feet hit the ground she was already spinning, ready to rush back to Robyn's side with the ball. She skidded to a stop, dropped the ball and zipped around Robyn's legs. Then she dashed off to line herself up for the next throw.

Robyn realised how lucky she was to have such a gorgeous dog. Paprika was so beautiful with her russet-brown coat shining in the afternoon sun. Her long tail curled high over her back, with its white-feathered tip fanned out. Paprika's eyes sparkled with excitement and her ears pricked. She was listening for the whoosh of rushing air overhead. Before the ball thudded on the ground, she was already turning towards the target.

When the others finally appeared on the beach, Robyn shouted to Paprika, "Go get Mum and Brad." Paprika whizzed past Robyn towards the rest of her pack and rounded them up.

"What took you guys so long?" Robyn asked.

"Had to get into my togs, dumbass," Brad said as he pulled a tongue at his big sister.

"Don't speak like that, Brad," Carol chastised him.

"Well, it was a dumb question."

"Enough! Let's just enjoy the beach," Carol said, to stop further argument from Brad, as she laid out the towels on the sand.

Robyn ran to the end of the beach, throwing the ball for Paprika every now and again. Brad followed but kept a few paces behind, still sulking after the reprimand. Once they returned to Carol they were hot and ready to get into the water. "Let's swim," Robyn said to Paprika. The dog was in the water like a flash, leaping over a small wave as it broke along the shore. "Beat you in, Brad," Robyn shouted as she sprinted into the water. She gasped. The cold water was a shock. She lifted her legs as high as she could in the shallows to boost her speed through the water. When it was deep enough, she dived head first through a small wave, otherwise she'd chicken out. As she surfaced, Brad moaned, "It's not fair, Robyn, you had a head start on me."

"Yes, I know – I cheated," she replied laughing, before diving back into the shimmering liquid. It didn't feel so cold now that her entire body was immersed. Paprika's legs churned to keep up with Robyn – the dog was faster on land but Robyn could pip her in the sea. "Mum, please throw the ball here?"

"Here you go, Robyn." And the game was on. Robyn put her head down and kicked as fast as her legs would go, stretching her arms at full reach. Robyn outswam Paprika by a good body-length, grabbed the ball and flung it close to Brad. Paprika whipped around, trying to grab her toy. But Brad threw himself at it and snatched it out of the air. He didn't want Paprika too close in case she knocked him with her teeth or claws. His bad mood forgotten now that he was playing in the water, he laughed and threw the ball back towards Robyn. The ball soared over Robyn's head into deeper water. As she turned towards it, she gasped in shock as she saw the fins of three large creatures. They were swimming parallel to the beach only about twenty metres away from her. Brad saw them at the same instant and shouted, "Look, Robyn, dolphins!"

Robyn's heart hammered in her ears. No way were those dolphins. They were in danger. She had to act fast.

CHAPTER SIX

Robyn's protective instinct took over. She raced for the ball. She plucked it out of the water and flung it as hard as she could towards the beach and yelled, "Paprika, fetch! Brad, get out of the water with Paprika. Now! Those aren't dolphins." She spun back to see one of the creatures heading directly towards them. Swimming for shallower water, she was thankful to see that Brad and Paprika had almost reached the safety of the beach. Her mother was shouting at Robyn to get out. Robyn's mind was racing. She knew these weren't sharks and was pretty sure they must be killer whales by the size of their fins. This was fantastic. To be so close to such majestic creatures was incredible. Her curiosity got the better of her and she stopped swimming. She was now able to stand and was only waist deep in the water, so she felt safe enough. One of them swam so close, she could see the white patch near its eyes, and the fin was unmistakably that of a killer whale.

Thank goodness, the whale turned and headed back to deeper water. Robyn realised with a jolt that it may have been after Paprika. She knew killer whales would almost beach themselves to catch seals. Maybe it had mistaken Paprika for a seal, or perhaps it was just curious. Or maybe a dog would have been an easy target in the water. Whatever the reason, Robyn was relieved she had acted fast to get Paprika out of the water.

Now that the shock was over, she stood in awe. Everyone else on the beach seemed to have stopped moving, mesmerised by these beautiful mammals. All three whales were now close together and appeared to be cruising in large circles. They surfaced, blowing plumes of fine mist. One of them threw itself into the air. It twisted and landed in an explosion of spray, churning up the water around it. Another whale breached, then the next. After that, for several seconds Robyn couldn't see them. They must have dived deeper. She squealed in delight as all three killer whales leapt into the air in unison. "Oh, wow – look at that." Their entire bodies shot out of the ocean. Then they smacked back into the water, sending huge columns of spray cascading into the air. And that was it – show over. The killer whales turned and swam off into the open ocean.

When they got home, Robyn took Paprika to the outside tap to wash the sand and salt water out of her coat. The hose-down wasn't Paprika's favourite activity but she stood still as Robyn sprayed her legs and underbelly with the hosepipe. Paprika lifted each foot in sequence for Robyn to rinse the sand off her paws. It seemed to Robyn that Paprika knew this was payment for her trip to the beach. After the hose-down, Paprika shook from head to foot then jumped into the back of the station wagon. Robyn rubbed her down with a towel, starting gently on her face. Then Paprika lifted her right paw and Robyn towelled her from her toes, up her leg and across her chest. Paprika's eyes went all soft and dreamy – she seemed to love this treatment. Then she lifted her left paw for the same indulgence. Robyn rubbed her tummy, back, tail and back legs. As soon as it was over, Paprika leapt out of the car. She tucked her back legs tight under her bum and propelled herself forward. She was like a crazy puppy, voicing little woofs to encourage Robyn to join her. Robyn wished she could do just that. It would be such fun. But on two legs she was no match for Paprika's quick twists and turns.

Later, Paprika watched Carol's every move as she prepared supper. "Do you want your dinner, Pappi?" Robyn asked as she joined her mother in the kitchen. Paprika looked up at Robyn with anticipation, ears pricked and head tilted to one side. "Okay, let's get you fed. One tablespoon of this yummy casserole, mmm nice dinner for my baby. Yuk! Glad it's for you and not me," she said, adding a scoop of doggie pellets. "Sit. Wait," Robyn commanded in a firm voice as she put the bowl on the floor. Paprika waited, holding her eyes on Robyn for the 'go' command. "Good girl, you can go."

"That's good timing," thought Robyn as she heard her father's car in the driveway just as Paprika finished eating. Paprika charged off through her doggie door to the gate, yapping with excitement. "Stop barking Paprika," Robyn yelled after her. Even though Paprika would be two years old in a couple of months, Robyn was still battling to stop this excited barking. Her mum had trained their previous dog, but Paprika was Robyn's responsibility as she had been Robyn's thirteenth birthday present last year. She was managing well with most of the training and the exercising, poop-scooping, washing, drying, brushing and feeding, but this barking was a problem. She'd have to work on it.

"Hey Paprika, what's all the noise about? It's just Daddy," Jim said as he bent down to give her a big hug. Hi Carol. Hi Robyn. Where's Brad? What's happening around here?" At that, Paprika ran off and returned with a ball in her mouth.

"Paprika still wants to play even though we took her to the beach for a run and swim. She's never had enough!" Robyn laughed.

Carol said, "Hi Jim, how was your day? Brad's upstairs doing his homework, I hope. If you're going up to see him, please check that he is doing his homework and not playing games on his iPad." Paprika rushed up the stairs after Jim. She was always looking for the action. But there wasn't any – Brad was in fact, in his room, doing his homework, much to Jim's surprise.

Paprika belted back downstairs and ran around the coffee table hoping to entice Robyn into a game. "Sorry girl. Have to get my hair dried now. We'll play later." This was the worst about having such thick, long hair, thought Robyn. Takes ages to dry. "Thank goodness you have a fine coat. Otherwise, with all the swimming you do, you'd be wet most of the time. And you stink when you're wet," Robyn said to Paprika, who cocked her head to the side, listening intently to Robyn's words in case 'play' was mentioned.

After dinner, Robyn asked Paprika, "Do you want to play hide and seek?" Paprika barked as though to say 'yes' and Robyn told her in a firm voice, "Wait." Paprika's sense of smell and hearing was incredible and Robyn was running out of new places to hide. She made a space inside her bedroom cupboard large enough to stand in with the door ajar. Then she whistled for Paprika. The dog raced up the stairs and sniffed around all the places Robyn usually hid. It didn't take her long to find the new hiding place and Robyn made a big fuss of her saying, "Good girl, Pappi. Clever dog." Paprika's tail wagged and she ran around excitedly. Robyn knew that she wanted more play.

After a few more rounds, Robyn took a dog biscuit out of the pantry. Paprika immediately rushed upstairs to her bed to wait for her bedtime treat. They had goodnight hugs and Paprika licked Robyn's hand. "Oh Pappi, I love you so much. Sleep well. See you in the morning."

Robyn looked over at Paprika before switching off her reading light. It was as though Paprika seemed to know that Robyn would check on her. Lifting an eyelid, she gazed at Robyn as though to wish her sweet dreams. Well, that's what it seemed like to Robyn.

And little did Robyn know just how sweet those dreams would be. And different... .

CHAPTER SEVEN

Robyn didn't understand what was happening. Everything was dark, except for a filtered light coming from one direction. Everything looked odd. She screamed as she realised she was deep underwater. But her scream didn't sound like her voice. And she didn't gag on water as she screamed. She wasn't craving for air. These revelations should have calmed her, but had the opposite effect. Her body tensed in alarm and she thrashed around in panic. Something brushed against her arm. No, it wasn't her arm. She didn't have an arm. She had... she had... a flipper! "Help, help," she screamed into the water. Again something touched her flipper. Instinct took over. She spun around, ready to defend herself in any way she could, without thought of what she might be about to face. She got the biggest surprise to see Paprika's distinctive amber eyes facing her.

"Relax Robyn. It's okay," Paprika said. Her dog spoke to her... in English! Oh no, Robyn thought – this was madness – her canine friend was talking to her. But as she looked into Paprika's eyes she felt her body relax. Paprika moved slightly away from Robyn, increasing the gap between them. Robyn could see more of her. In fact, she could see her completely. Now this was seriously crazy. Either her mind was playing tricks on her or she was dreaming. Her dog wasn't a dog, she was a penguin. Then it dawned on Robyn that, as she also had a flipper instead of an arm, she must be a penguin too. Crazy, crazy, crazy. "Paprika, what's happening? Have I gone nuts?"

"No Robyn, you are okay. We're just penguins chilling down here in the Antarctic."

"What's happened to my dog? What's happened to me? Where's my family? Why are we are penguins? What are we doing in the Antarctic? How come you can talk to me?" Questions poured out of Robyn in confusion and alarm.

"Relax Robyn. Everything is going to be all right. Haha, now I get to call the shots for a change. You're always telling me to relax. So, I can talk to you because I'm so clever – remember, that's what you say? Anyway, I digress. Your family is safe and sound at home, and we are going to be back with them later. Don't worry, just enjoy yourself."

"But why are we penguins? And why are we here?" Robyn continued in a shrill voice.

"Oh for goodness sake Robyn, stop panicking. Relax, have fun, take some risks for a change. You are such a worry machine. You should just chill and live for the moment."

"Well, okay I'll try," Robyn said as she attempted to moderate her tone of voice and slow her breathing. "But right now, I think I need some air."

"Good idea, follow me," replied Paprika as she sped up towards the light with a few flicks of her flippers. Robyn flapped and jerked. And she flapped and jerked... and flapped and jerked. She was hardly moving. She was trying hard to keep up with Paprika who seemed to glide effortlessly through the water. But it sure wasn't working. "Robyn – stop fighting. You look like my teddy bear when I throw it around. You know the one that had all that lovely stuffing that I pulled out and dumped all over the floor? Yeah, you look just like that unstuffed teddy, with floppy limbs all over the place. You know you are just wasting energy like that. Use smooth, easy strokes with your flippers, like this."

Robyn laughed at the analogy of her dog's torn toy. She watched Paprika carefully. She slowed her movements and caressed the water with her flippers. Immediately her body flowed through the water and her speed increased. That was more like it. Now her swimming was smooth, and she was making headway.

"Wow, this is cool." She exhaled as she joined Paprika on the surface and took a large breath of polar air. She didn't feel the cold bite into her lungs. That was odd. Her body was warm and comfortable. Then Robyn remembered reading that penguins had many layers of feathers to keep them warm. The oiled and waterproofed outer layer was keeping her dry.

"I'm glad you got the hang of that fast. You looked ridiculous when you first tried to swim," Paprika mocked Robyn.

"Like you did when you first got knocked over by a wave at the beach as a puppy and didn't know which way was up or down?" Robyn quipped back at her.

Paprika let out a chuckle. "Yes, I guess just like that."

"So now I know how, let's swim – I want to go as fast as I can. Let's race."

"Okay, game on," Paprika yelled as she ducked under the water and torpedoed through the cold liquid world. Robyn flapped hard, propelling herself after her friend. Paprika made a sudden right turn and Robyn sped past her. Oh no, Paprika hadn't told her how to turn. Paprika looped over and launched her streamlined body after Robyn. "Watch how I use my feet and tail as a rudder," she urged. Then she was twisting and turning effortlessly. Her little tail moved from side to side and up and down, directing her passage. Robyn couldn't quite tell how

Paprika was using her feet. Most of the time they just stuck out behind her, almost touching. Now and again they splayed outwards. It was hard to figure out.

Robyn decided the best way to learn was to try. She moved her lower body to the left. Oops, too much. She almost stopped. Gradually she got more co-ordination. She began to use the right amount of tail and feet movement to get her body to turn at the angle she wanted. After a few more trips to the surface for air and some practice moves, she knew she was swimming with almost as much ease and elegance as Paprika. "This is fantastic," Robyn squealed with delight. "I've always loved being in the water, but this is the ultimate. It feels wonderful going so fast and being able to manoeuvre like that. You move beautifully in the water in a penguin's body. As good as you look when you are on land in your dog's body, Pappi." With a chuckle, she added, "And you're heaps faster in the water now than you are as a dog."

"Yes, it's easier being a penguin in water than a dog. I wanted to show you how good life is here – so unspoiled by humans. I don't mean to offend you. I mean humans in general. Humans ruin this beautiful planet. But enough of that – we are here to have fun and enjoy being penguins. Keep close to me." Paprika boosted away again, rolling, spinning, flipping and flapping, and just plain showing off. Robyn tried to copy her moves and impressed herself, as she managed it with no further problem. They played tag. They managed beautiful acrobatic moves in the clear water. They dived deep and then zoomed back up to the surface like rockets.

After several minutes of fooling around, Paprika pointed out a mass of krill. "Let's grab some lunch."

"What a great idea, I'm starving after all that exercise," Robyn agreed. In that instant, she realised she could actually smell the salty sea life and fish. "Hey, Pappi, all of a sudden I don't mind the smell of fish. Smells delicious, and you know how I usually loathe it?" And with that, she copied Paprika and attacked the small crustaceans with gusto. They tasted incredible, especially when washed down with a good swig of seawater.

"Food fit for kings of the Antarctic," said Paprika. She nudged Robyn. "I hope you got that... you do know that we are King Penguins, don't you?"

"Yes, I do. And I knew you had a sense of humour," Robyn giggled.

"Okay, Robyn, we're going onto the ice now. There is a bit of a ledge to get up. You need to go fast towards it, then propel yourself up and out of the water before you scramble up onto the ice. Watch how I do it. It can take a bit of practice to get the timing right."

Robyn could see the ice looming nearer. It was daunting. She'd just got the hang of the swimming. Now she was expected to throw herself out of the water and onto the ice. She watched in awe as Paprika put on some speed and flew out of the water. Robyn could see her plop gently onto the ice. Then she was flapping like crazy to shift up the incline without slipping back down. Robyn swam in circles below the ice, unsure of what to do. It sounded and looked easy when Paprika did it, but could she manage it? Robyn wasn't feeling confident. What if she hit the shelf? What if she banged too hard on the ice? What if she made it only to slip back down? How many times would she have to attempt it? Her confidence had completely disappeared. She felt bewildered and unsure of herself and wished that Paprika hadn't left her here alone.

Robyn felt a sudden rush of water around her. She was no longer alone. Dozens and dozens of penguins swam past her towards the ice, leaping up at different times. Some fell back into the water, unsuccessful in their attempts. Others disappeared from view into the mass of penguins already on the ice. They all seemed to be in a mad rush to get out of the water and onto the frozen mass above. Then Robyn heard Paprika cry out in alarm, "Come on Robyn, quick. Leap onto the ice. There's a leopard seal in the water."

Robyn knew this deadly predator had razor-like teeth and unyielding jaws. It would take out a little penguin in an instant. Especially a novice like her. She had no idea how to outwit a seal.

With a cry of anguish, Robyn spun around. The seal was moving at high speed towards her. There was no way she had time to attempt that hurdle onto the ice now. If she missed, she was bound to fall into the gaping jaws of the menacing seal. She did the only other thing she could. With her heart banging loudly in her chest, she turned away. She beat her flippers as fast as she could, trying to get some distance between herself and the looming monster. She was in its sights. It was after her. She thought her heart would burst right out of her body, it was pumping so hard and fast.

She shrieked, "Help Paprika, help me." But even as she cried out, she knew her friend couldn't help. Robyn dived deeper into the water. The seal was gaining on her. She felt the water quiver near her tail. Then there was a quick sharp pain in her left foot. Instinctively she put on an extra burst of speed. Luck was with her as she cleared herself away from the seal's snapping jaws. At that instant she sensed a large shape moving up fast from the depths of the ocean. The water surged around her as her body rocked in sudden turbulence. Something huge was near. She was so scared and disoriented, her mind couldn't even consider what it could be. She realised she was in mortal danger. So, this was it. Her end was here. She was going to die in the Antarctic.

CHAPTER EIGHT

To Robyn's surprise and relief, the seal veered away from her. It must know what was approaching. It must be terrified by the other creature near them. Otherwise it wouldn't have stopped the chase. What a turnaround. Now the hunter became the hunted as a killer whale homed in on the leopard seal. Robyn exhaled in relief as she realised how close she had been to certain death.

With her heart still pounding, she whipped around and swam as fast as she could away from the hunters. She surfaced for a breath of much-needed air and hoped to glimpse her friend. She quickly rotated to scan the ice. And just a short distance away was a mass of colour – the bright yellow and orange markings so distinctive of the king penguins. She ducked under the water and headed for the sanctuary of the ice and the companionship of her kind. She sighed with relief as she saw Paprika and another penguin racing towards her.

"Oh Robyn, I'm so sorry. I was supposed to look after you and show you how wonderful this place is, not get you into danger. I thought I was going to lose you. I'm so sorry," Paprika said.

"I'm okay, Pappi. Lucky I'm such a good swimmer,"

Robyn replied with a forced grin. She tried to make light of the situation to ease her friend's guilt. "Just got a nip on my left little toe. Look it's nothing – just a scratch. Thank goodness the killer whale was alone. Otherwise, I may have been a killer whale's meal. I guess if the leopard seal hadn't been so close to me, I would have been the killer whale's target. But lucky for me, a big fat seal must have made a more tantalising dinner menu than a scrawny penguin. Lesson learned though. Next time you suggest I try something, like leaping out of the water onto the ice, I won't be such a wimp. I'll just go for it. Let's try it now so I won't hesitate ever again."

"Good idea. Robyn, this is Gwen. We've known each other a long time. Gwen, please will you go ahead and show Robyn how you get yourself up onto the ice?" Paprika asked. "I will follow with her."

"Hi Robyn, it's good to meet you finally. Rika has told me lots about you and her plans for you. Let's get out of here." With that Gwen spun around and raced back to the ice before Robyn had a chance to ask what she meant about plans. Robyn and Paprika followed Gwen. They reached her just as she neared the ice shelf where the penguin colony was basking in the sun. "I prefer to go a bit deeper first so I get a real boost to launch myself high into the air like this," Gwen shouted. She dived under the water and looped up. She soared through the air so high and far, landing on top of another penguin relaxing in the sun.

"Hey, watch out Gwen. You know I love you, but I'd rather you didn't squash me," the penguin wheezed.

"Oops, sorry Burt... thought you'd enjoy a hug," Gwen replied with a cheeky grin.

"Show off," Paprika yelled with a laugh. "Okay, Robyn let's go. Dive down then go as fast as you can to the surface. Swim right beside me, so you'll get the angle and timing correct." They dived down and, making a 'u' shape in the water, raced up towards the ice sheet. When they were almost underneath the overhang, they flicked themselves up and out. They both landed on their feet on the ice.

"Amazing, I did it!" whooped Robyn as she tried unsuccessfully to clap with her flippers. There were hundreds of penguins on the ice, and they all seemed to be standing upright with beaks raised in the air. They looked like absolute snobs, looking down their beaks at everyone else. But they were beautiful. Their feathers were sleek, and their chests shone pearly-white in the bright sunlight. The contrast of their colour was exquisite against the glaring ice. They looked regal with their long white shirts, blue-black tuxedo jackets, and orange and yellow bibs and beaks. Their eyes were so dark it was hard to make them out, except when the light caught them. Paprika's amber dog-eyes looked strange on her penguin face. But it made her easy to recognise among the other penguins. She also had a white tip on her little tail, like Paprika the dog had. Robyn giggled. She imagined how weird Paprika would look if her penguin tail was as long and hairy as her dog tail. "Oh boy," Robyn thought aloud, "I'm definitely going mad."

"It's time to catch up, Robyn," said Gwen as she turned away from the penguin crowds. Robyn took one step to follow. And promptly fell flat on her face.

Paprika roared with laughter, "Oh my goodness, that's hilarious Robyn. You can't even walk."

"Oh, hilarious. Easy for you. You've done this before," she replied indignantly. And then she saw the funny side of it and burst out laughing too. "I feel like I forgot to pull up my pants after going to the loo. Now they're down around my ankles, tripping me up. So, clever one. How do I get up now that I'm flat on my feathery belly?" she asked, grinning.

"Carefully," chirped Paprika with a twinkle in her eye.

"Thanks, that helps heaps," Robyn shot back. She was still lying awkwardly on her stomach.

"Okay, I'll stop teasing you, now I've had a good laugh at your expense. Put your feet under you. Then push yourself up using your flippers. Use your tail to help you balance. Then take small steps as though I've tied your legs together below your knees. Hold your flippers out at your side and direct them backwards a little. You'll be running before you know it," explained Paprika as her laughter subsided.

"This is so much harder than swimming. I feel so clumsy," muttered Robyn.

"You'll get used to it," Gwen encouraged. "We love to slide on our bellies, especially if there's a slope like this to go down. Let's give it a go," she suggested.

"Sounds like fun, providing I can make the long hike up the slope on these stubby legs," Robyn replied.

"We'll saunter up there so you can keep up. I haven't tobogganed for a while. It'll be fun to do it again," Gwen added.

Robyn watched Gwen and Paprika for a few seconds as they waddled up the slope. She thought they looked as awkward on land as they were graceful in the sea. Robyn took a tentative step to follow them, and then another. Her body seemed to rock from side to side as she walked and it felt ridiculous. She concentrated on taking small steps and using her flippers and tail for balance. Soon she got into a rhythm. But she wasn't about to try to race after the others. They had already reached the top of the slope. They said they would saunter – so much for that. But if she hurried she'd no doubt fall on her face again and they'd just laugh at her.

Robyn traipsed on at what felt to her like a snail's pace. Finally, she reached the top without falling on her face again. Or on her butt. The top of the slope was much higher than she expected. The icy vista spread all around her, as far as she could see. It was so calm and pure and unspoiled. Robyn marvelled at the scene and whispered, "This is amazing – it's so tranquil. And it goes on forever.

The silence and peace are breathtaking."

"It's wonderful, isn't it?" agreed Paprika.

"Yes, and it's weird because I feel like I belong here. I've got to admit that the waddle is pretty odd, but otherwise it's like being home. Even after that seal chased me, I feel as though I'm safe and where I'm supposed to be. I know this isn't real. I belong in a human body, living with my human family, with my human feet firmly planted on the ground. But right now, this seems right. It's so strange," Robyn said.

"I knew you'd get it, Robyn. Didn't I tell you she was the right person, Gwen?"

"You sure did," Gwen nodded.

"Robyn, I knew you'd appreciate this beautiful place. The tranquil beauty and the perfect balance of nature are very evident here. By comparison, some of the human world is warped. Warped by opinions, greed, mistrust, envy, corruption and power struggles. And that's just a few of the issues. But, I don't want to get morbid on you. We are here to have fun – follow me," Paprika responded. She faced downhill and threw herself onto her belly.

Robyn followed. Copying Paprika, she pushed with feet and flippers until momentum and gravity took over. Next thing they were careening down towards the edge of the ice and the sea beyond. Gwen overtook them with a Tarzan yell. Then they were shrieking and whooping with delight as they dived off the small cliff into the icy sea. Plummeting into the clear depths of the Southern Ocean, they were once again nimble and supple in their watery world.

Robyn's pulse raced with excitement and exertion as they frolicked in the water. They cavorted around playing catch with great gusto then finally slowed to rest. Robyn felt so at peace and in tune with her body in this idyllic place. As Paprika glided towards her, Robyn said, "What did you mean when you said to Gwen that I was the right person?"

Paprika didn't answer her. Instead, she looked directly into Robyn's eyes. There was a peculiar intensity in her gaze that sent Robyn reeling. The amber of Paprika's eyes became Robyn's entire focus. Then she felt a strange sensation as though she was spinning out of control. There was a shrill, insistent buzzing sound all around her.

CHAPTER NINE

Robyn jolted awake to the annoying buzzing of her cellphone. As she rolled over to switch off the alarm, Paprika nudged her gently with her nose to say good morning. "Hi, Pappi, how's my gorgeous girl?" Robyn asked as she stroked Paprika's ears. "Did you sleep well? I did." As she got out of bed Robyn realised she felt rested and energetic this morning. "Come, let's go." Paprika's ears pricked up – she was always ready for action.

As Robyn was about to put on her running shoes, she noticed a small scratch on her left baby toe. As she leaned over to inspect it, Paprika licked her toes. Robyn giggled as it tickled when Paprika did that. Robyn couldn't remember what she had done to get that scratch on her toe. She thought maybe Paprika had caught it when they were swimming yesterday. It wasn't bleeding or sore, so she ignored it, and continued getting dressed. Once she was ready, she headed downstairs, Paprika by her side.

"Morning Robyn," said her mum as she gave Robyn a hug. "Are you taking Paprika for a walk before school?"

"Hi Mum, we're leaving in a few minutes. Outside Paprika, go toilet." Paprika responded immediately by going outside through the doggy door. "Good girl," said

Robyn when Paprika returned to the kitchen. Paprika waited beside the cupboard for the biscuit she knew she would get. "Sit. Paw," Robyn said as she offered a biscuit to Paprika. "Good girl, now take it to your bed." Paprika took her biscuit to eat on her blanket under the stairs. After she had finished it, she ran back to Robyn, watching her expectantly. "Do you want to go for a run?" Robyn asked. Paprika's eyes lit up and, with ears up and forward, she gave a short bark, which Robyn knew was her way of saying yes. Robyn attached the lead to Paprika's collar and headed towards the front door. "Bye Mum, we'll be back in about twenty minutes."

Paprika jogged beside Robyn and helped her keep a good pace up the hills. Paprika's bright eyes observed everything around her. She showed her interest in the way she held her tail high and wagged it. Robyn loved these times with her canine companion who made her feel safe and loved. Paprika was great to exercise with as Robyn chose the pace. Sometimes when she ran with friends their pace would be too slow, or they would complain about the hills. Not Paprika – she was game for everything.

On their return home, they were both thirsty and had good long drinks of water. Robyn fed Paprika and filled a bowl with cereal for herself. Paprika followed her to the bedroom after Robyn had showered. She watched Robyn's every move and got excited when Robyn sat in front of her mirror. Whenever Robyn was at her dressing table, Paprika was on full alert. Her head moved from side to side, checking the walls and floor for reflections. She loved to chase the shimmering lights. The family referred to this game as 'sparkles', and it was one of Paprika's favourites. This morning the sunlight was streaming through the bedroom window. Robyn picked up the mirror. She pulled a face as she tied up her thick blonde hair and scrutinised her reflection. "Oh, Pappi, I look so pale and washed out. I hate my pasty skin. I look like a ghost." Paprika yapped at Robyn and pawed the air. Robyn laughed and shook the mirror from side to side. "You're so demanding. Okay, here are some sparkles for you."

Paprika pounced on the glints of light, rushing after the dazzling target. Robyn moved the reflection around the room, being careful not to shine it in the dog's eyes. Paprika was besotted with sparkles to the point where it was all-consuming. Jim had removed his weather station from the back garden because of Paprika's obsession. The weather station's wind direction unit, which looked like a jet plane, had become an issue. When the sun was shining, Paprika fixated on the reflections along the side of the house and bushes. When playing this game, she wouldn't respond when called. She didn't even greet the family when they arrived home. All she wanted to do was chase the sparkles. Although it was good exercise for her, it was an unhealthy obsession for the dog's mind. So Robyn kept the sparkle game to a minimum. That didn't stop Paprika being forever optimistic.

This morning, after a minute or so of playing the game, Robyn said, "Okay, Pappi, that's enough. I've got to go now. Come give me a big hug." Paprika ignored her, still intent on looking for sparkles. But when Robyn got up, grabbed her school bag and started for the bedroom door, Paprika was hot on her heels. She knew the routine and ran downstairs, waiting for Robyn to catch up to her. They had a big cuddle, and then Robyn said, "Bye Paprika, bye Mum. See you later."

Jim had already left for work and had dropped Brad off at school on his way to work. Carol worked from home most of the time. She had landed a contract with a web-design company in the city. She only had to go into their offices now and again for meetings and to discuss projects, so Paprika was lucky that she wasn't left alone too often. Paprika sat at the gate watching until Robyn was out of sight. Robyn knew that Paprika would now find a spot in the sun and lie down for a snooze.

Robyn had mixed feelings today. She was dreading

another ghastly day at school, but at least Hayley was back, plus she had a weird feeling of excitement. Last night she was fretting about an essay they had to write today. They had no information on the topic so couldn't do any research. "Weird," she thought, as she tried to analyse why she was okay with it today. Usually, she had a knot in her stomach from worry about writing essays. But today was different. It was almost as though she had excited butterflies. Maybe there was something else causing these feelings? She couldn't think of anything. Oh well, it was good to be feeling this way for a change.

Maybe today was going to be a good day after all.

CHAPTER TEN

Hayley was already on the bus. She was sitting next to a boy Robyn hadn't seen before. Robyn was disappointed because she wanted to sit with Hayley so she could tell her about her horrible last week. With Hayley arriving home so late last night, Robyn hadn't even been able to speak to her yet. But it was probably better that she wasn't able to talk to her about it now – a bus wasn't an ideal place to have a private conversation. She would have to pretend that everything was okay, as she didn't want Hayley asking questions in front of the others. But just having Hayley back made Robyn feel better.

As Robyn sat across the aisle from them, she grinned and asked, "Hi Hayley, how was the holiday? Sounded fantastic from what you messaged to me. But I'm looking forward to hearing more about it. I'm so glad to have you back. You have no idea how much I missed you."

"Hi Robyn, I missed you too. I had a great time, and it was so lovely for my grandmother to have all the family with her for her seventieth birthday. I will tell you about it later. Robyn, this is Tamati. His family has just moved from Christchurch, and they are now living next door to me. Tamati, this is my best friend, Robyn."

"Hi. It's nice to meet you Tamati. Are you settling in okay?" Robyn greeted him with a smile.

"Hi Robyn, yes it's good so far thanks," he replied.

"So, what brings you to the big city?" Robyn asked.

"My dad got a company promotion and they transferred him here. He's sweet as about it. He's wanted to move us all to Auckland for a while."

"It's Tamati's first day at our school today. We'll have to look after him and pay him special attention," said Hayley with a twinkle in her eye. "Hopefully, you'll be in most of our classes Tamati."

Just then the bus stopped and several noisy teenagers got on. There were five boys and two girls in the group. "They look lively so early in the morning," remarked Tamati.

"They're on the gymnastics team and they've been out training already, so they are all on a high. They're always way too happy so early in the morning," moaned Hayley, pulling a face.

"Don't be such a grump Hayley. Maybe if you got up earlier and did some exercise, you wouldn't be so miserable in the mornings," Robyn said with a giggle. "They're nice."

"Yeah, they're okay. Not like Gina and her gang," Hayley responded with a grimace.

Robyn and Hayley knew one of the boys from the team, as he was in their science class. "Hey girls," he said as he sat on the seat in front of Robyn.

"Hi Ryan, did you have a good workout?" Robyn asked.

"Yeah thanks, it was great. I learned to do a new trick today, which has been challenging. I have been battling with it for ages. I keep watching it done by the pros on YouTube, and it looks easy. But all I've got so far are the bruises from all my mistakes," Ryan replied, grinning.

"That's cool, well done. Maybe that'll be the end of the bruises, from that trick anyway," Robyn responded. "Ryan this is Tamati who's starting school here today. Tamati –

Ryan."

The boys greeted each other and then a few of Ryan's team started singing at the tops of their voices. Robyn couldn't hear herself think, let alone speak. All at once the boys fell silent, with necks craned, checking out the girls at the next bus stop. Hayley leaned across the aisle and whispered to Robyn, "Boys are so predictable. Look at them eyeing that lot like they are their next meal."

Robyn could see the attraction. Gina and her friends were good looking. But they could be malicious to others who weren't part of their cool group. Robyn knew first-hand. She'd been on the receiving end since Hayley had been away. She didn't even want to think about it now. It would just spoil the perfect beginning to her day. To take her mind off it she asked Ryan, "So what was the trick you mastered today, Ryan?"

Just as Ryan was about to reply, Gina sidled up close to him, pushing his butt over on the seat with her own. "Hey Ryan, shift up. Or I can sit on your lap if you prefer," Gina said as she batted her eyelashes at Ryan. Gina immediately won Ryan's attention as he moved over on the seat. Robyn had to admit that Gina was stunning. Her hair was dark brown and shiny, and her olive skin evenly tanned. Her eyes were so dark they were almost black, and framed by gorgeous thick dark lashes. She had curves in all the right places and a deep husky voice. Despite herself, Robyn was a little envious of Gina's looks. But Gina could be spiteful and manipulative, and she flirted unashamedly with any of the boys that she liked the look of. She certainly didn't seem to give a damn about anyone else's feelings.

Robyn outwardly ignored the way Gina had butted in on her and Ryan. She tried to tell herself that she should not be troubled by Gina. But she was battling. After all, Gina had made her life hell for the past few days. Robyn could feel tears pricking behind her eyes. She told herself to calm down. But Gina had managed to sour Robyn's day before the day had hardly begun. It was evident to Robyn that Gina intended exactly that, as she turned in her seat and smirked at Robyn. Then Gina swivelled back to Ryan and whispered something in his ear. Robyn couldn't hear, but she thought it would be something derogatory about her. At least Ryan didn't seem to react to the comment.

Hayley reached across the aisle and patted Robyn's leg. She gave her a big grin as she batted her eyelashes, mimicking Gina. Robyn giggled and immediately relaxed. Her best friend had a way of knowing how to calm her. Hayley was such a carefree person who didn't let things get to her. She just seemed to be able to brush things off, which was something Robyn had trouble doing. Robyn took way too much to heart. Although Robyn had called Hayley 'grumpy' a few minutes ago, it was a joke between them. Hayley was seldom grumpy – she just liked to comment on what she saw. It made her fun to be around as she was always making remarks about how people looked and acted. It wasn't malicious. Hayley just liked to voice her observations, and they were often entertaining.

When the bus stopped at school and Ryan stood up, Gina grabbed his hand and pulled him into the aisle. She yanked him along with her towards the front of the bus. Ryan turned back to Robyn with a raised eyebrow. "Cheers Robyn, see you later."

Robyn smiled at him as she picked up her bag. "Sure, see you at Science." She immediately felt her good mood return.

It was shaping up to be an interesting day.

CHAPTER ELEVEN

Robyn, Hayley and Tamati walked to their first class together. Tamati had registered at school the previous week, so he knew what classes he would be attending. As they were walking through the corridor, Robyn noticed how big Tamati was. He towered over the girls, with strong, broad shoulders, big biceps and muscular legs. He was good-looking and had a captivating presence. He exuded confidence, yet seemed natural and unassuming in his manner. It was as though he didn't realise the effect that he had on others as all heads turned towards him. Girls in the corridor whispered and nudged each other as they spotted him. The guys looked impressed, and maybe a bit envious. Tamati smiled at everyone as he passed them. Hayley whispered to Robyn, "I think Tamati is making an impression." Then to Tamati, "Here are the lockers. Did the office give you a number?"

"Yes, 303," answered Tamati as he found the locker. He opened it to check it was empty, then fumbled around in his backpack. He pulled out a few items and put them in the locker and then secured it shut with his padlock. By the time he'd finished messing around most of the students had gone to their classes.

As they entered the classroom, Hayley introduced Tamati to their English teacher, Mrs Watkins. She welcomed him. Then in a loud voice to rise above the chatter of the students, she called, "Attention everyone, please welcome Tamati."

The room immediately went quiet as the teenagers checked out the new boy in town. Almost in unison, they said, "Hi Tamati." There was a lot of whispering and scraping of chairs as the trio made their way to the third row. They were fortunate to find three seats together.

"Okay class, settle down and let's begin. Phones away and on silent please," said Mrs Watkins as she brought up a document from her laptop onto the large screen at the front of the classroom. "I mentioned before that you would be writing an essay today, but didn't give you a subject. You can write about anything that relates to the partial sentence on the screen. The essay should, of course, include good grammar and spelling. But what I want you to concentrate on is bringing feelings and some action into your writing. As you can see, the sentence begins, *What would life be if...* . That should give you plenty of scope, so there's no excuse for not giving me some exceptional work. You should write between five hundred and a thousand words, but that's just a guide. Your primary objectives are good content and expression. You may begin now."

There were a few groans and sighs around the classroom. There was lots of fidgeting and scraping of chairs and clearing of throats. Finally, the students settled in front of their computer screens.

Robyn grinned to herself as she realised that, somehow, she knew what subject she was going to choose. She didn't have to sit and rack her brains as usual. It was as though the words were about to burst out of her head. Thank goodness she was a fast typist, as she had lots to say, and quickly. Even so, she was surprised how easily the first words appeared on her screen. 'Gwen and the other beautiful king penguins glided through the icy waters of the Antarctic.' Robyn seemed to know how a penguin would feel as it swam gracefully and effortlessly in the Antarctic Ocean. Her ideas were vivid as they sprung into her mind. It was as though she was watching a movie. No – she was, in fact, part of the movie. It was as though she was there. She could smell the salt and feel the cold air on her nose as she came up for breath. She knew what food she had to find. She knew how it would feel to leap out of the water onto the ice shelf. She knew she had to take little steps to waddle on the icy continent. It was a strange sensation. She decided not to question it. She told herself to go with the flow. She was thankful that she was finding it so easy to express herself for a change. By the end of the lesson, she had hammered out 912 words and even had time to check for errors. Unbelievable. It was usual for her to spend much of the time sitting staring at the screen, anxious that she couldn't get words down. Then she would panic at the end as she couldn't finish in time. Robyn felt elated and hoped the rest of the day would prove to be as easy.

"Well done, class. Time's up. Please save your work. You will have your results next week. No homework tonight as I'm sure you've had enough English for one day," Mrs Watkins said as she opened the classroom door.

As Hayley stood, she said, "Whew, no homework for a change. What happened to you? I've never seen you type so flat out and be so focused. You scared me. Who are you and what have you done with Robyn?"

Robyn laughed. "I don't know what got into me. But it was awesome that for once I actually knew what I was doing."

"Yay, it's about time. You always work so hard and panic too much – you've earned some slack," Hayley responded supportively. "That wasn't a bad topic – as Mrs Watkins said, it gave us scope. I wrote about how life would be if I was a pop star. What did you write about?"

"What life would be like as a penguin," Robyn said.

"What the... that's seriously weird. Where on earth did that come from?" Hayley asked with an amused expression on her face.

"I have no idea. I know it's bizarre," Robyn returned with a giggle. "Anyway, let's get moving otherwise we are going to be late for Geography."

"Will I see you later at Science?" asked Tamati.

"Sure," answered Robyn and Hayley together.

"Catch you later," said Hayley as the girls headed for their geography class.

As they were out of earshot, Hayley added, "Oh my goodness isn't he just gorgeous?"

"Yeah, he seems nice," said Robyn.

"Nice? Nice? Didn't you notice that body? And his face?" Hayley squealed, astounded at her friend's apparent lack of observation.

"Of course I noticed. But more important is that Tamati seems nice," Robyn returned with a grin.

"Yeah, he's nice... but that body is something else! The other boys look like wimps in comparison," Hayley insisted.

Robyn giggled, elbowed Hayley, then she whispered. "I need to talk to you Hayley. It's about Gina. I can't explain now, but you have no idea how good it is to have you back."

As they walked into their next class, Gina and her gang were all whispering. They were sending dagger looks at Hayley who gave them a big grin and walked to her seat with a cocky bounce in her step. Robyn recognised her friend's attitude. It was Hayley's way of letting the others know that they didn't get to her and that she was up for a challenge if that's what they wanted. Gina's bunch must have sensed it too as they stopped whispering and looked away. Robyn doubted that Gina would leave Hayley's challenge at that, though. And Hayley didn't even know yet what had happened while she was away.

For Robyn the rest of the day flew by. She was in a good mood after managing her essay without an issue, and with having her friend back. Hayley seemed to be in a great mood. She was joking and teasing light-heartedly with their friends. It was definitely one of the better days at school. Robyn was surprised how soon the school day had come to an end. And as a double bonus, they had no homework this weekend.

Hopefully she'd have a good night's sleep tonight. Tomorrow was going to be busy, and she had Hayley's birthday party to look forward to in the evening.

CHAPTER TWELVE

"Robyn, wait up," cried Brad. Robyn opened her eyes to see a polar bear cub bounding across the snow towards her. She yelled, "Brad! Hurry, we've got to get out of here in case the mother bear is nearby." She reached out to grab Brad's hand to steer him away from the danger, but her hand didn't find his. As she turned to look for Brad her heart raced. Standing on its hind legs, only metres from her, was a huge adult polar bear. Robyn screamed. She was about to run when her eyes met the bear's. She realised in an instant that those amber eyes were unmistakably Paprika's. Robyn looked down at her own legs. She was standing on four, almost white, fluffy legs, with long claws at their tips. "This is crazy," she muttered as she realised she must be a bear cub. And the other cub must be Brad.

"Hi Robyn, welcome to the Arctic. This time I thought it would be fun to have Brad with us," said Paprika.

"Oh, thank goodness it's you," replied Robyn as her breathing returned to normal. The hammering in her chest slowed down and her sense of humour returned. "So, you have turned the tables on me again. I suppose I will have to take orders from you again?" Robyn questioned with a giggle.

"Yes, that's right," answered Paprika. "It's a mother's job to keep her young safe, so you must obey me for your own safety," she added in a no-nonsense tone, sounding just like Robyn's mother. "You cubs have lots to learn. Bear cubs are only protected by their mother for a couple of years and then they're on their own."

"Brad, come here," Robyn commanded.

"You know Robyn, you're prettier as a polar bear, but you're still so bossy. And now that you aren't my big sister, you can't tell me what to do," Brad laughed. He stood on his hind legs and puffed out his hairy chest.

"Haha, I guess that's true," replied Robyn as she ran after the mother polar bear.

"Come on you two, let's go hunting seals. You need lots of calories to grow. The seal meat and blubber help build up fat reserves to keep you warm and healthy. At the moment you're still getting that from my milk, but you need to start eating meat as well. When seal hunting isn't good, we'll have to resort to eating other things, like fish, rodents and plants, and whatever else we can find to keep us alive. But the best meal by a long shot is a seal."

Robyn and Brad rushed after their mother with excitement. Paprika asked, "What can you smell right now?"

"Your yummy milk," replied Brad.

"Fair enough, but that wasn't the answer I wanted. Take in a deep breath through your nose. Now concentrate on what other smells are out there," Paprika suggested. Both cubs inhaled deeply. Their eyes grew wider with delight at all the new smells they hadn't noticed before. The crisp air was tainted with salt and delicious aromas. Their mother told them that was a sure sign that seals were nearby.

"Ooh," sighed Brad, "that smells good, let's go get us a seal."

Paprika stopped. "Shh, be quiet," she told the cubs.

She tracked stealthily across the ice, and the cubs slunk behind her. Their mother stopped at a small hole in the ice. She explained in a whisper, "This is a seal's breathing hole. We must wait patiently for a seal to come up for air." She stood motionless, intent on the dark hole. The cubs tried to mimic their mother but within a few minutes boredom set in. They became restless. They started bumping into each other. They hit each other with their front paws. Next thing they were rolling around causing a commotion.

Paprika huffed, "Oh, well done Robyn and Brad. You scared the seal away. Now we will have to start all over again at another hole. It will be too wary to try this breathing hole again now. So, you can sniff out the next hole. Let's move on." Paprika instructed sternly.

They walked. And they walked. And they walked, for what seemed like hours to Robyn. The cubs tried to sniff out seal breathing-holes but they were hopeless at it. Eventually, Brad cried out, "I smell one." He charged towards the hole in the ice.

"Slow down Brad. And be quiet. Pad to the hole. You don't want to scare this seal off too, do you?" asked Paprika. "You've missed four holes before you found this one. You need to pay more attention. Finding food isn't a game. One seal will keep us going for about a week. When we get closer, you two stay back and be still. I will wait at the hole in the hope that a nearby seal needs air soon. Be patient – it could take time. Lie down and rest, but be attentive. Don't fall asleep as you don't want to miss the lesson."

Both cubs were tired and hungry, so they responded at once to their mother's instruction. They moved a few metres away from the hole and lay down, watching their mother with interest. They were hungry now and looked forward to trying some seal. This time they were lucky. They only had to wait a few minutes for the action. All of a sudden their mother leaned right back on her haunches, then threw herself towards the hole. As the seal surfaced, the bear struck it hard and dragged it out of the water. Robyn's human brain was horrified at the savagery and brute strength of the mother bear. At the same time, she realised that the seal had died in an instant so it wouldn't have suffered too much. Robyn knew this was the cycle of life, and the violence was only necessary to sustain life. It was all part of an intricate and finely balanced system.

"Come and eat," said the mother polar bear as she dragged the dead seal towards the cubs. Robyn's animal instincts took over. She was hungry, and the smell of the fresh meat was tantalising. She got stuck in with the others. Her first taste of the raw meat was delicious.

Once they had all eaten their fill, Paprika explained a little about the survival of polar bears. "The predators of polar bears are humans and other polar bears. We can also starve to death, or die from an injury inflicted by other polar bears. As young cubs, we also have to watch out for wolves. The Earth's pollution and global warming affect the environment. With the melting icecaps, we have less hunting ground. Also, as people hunt for seals, it results in less food for us. People used to hunt us but we are now protected by government laws. However, there are still those who would kill us, so humans can't be trusted. Although polar bears are the top dogs in the Arctic, we have to be aware of everything around us. Survival is tough."

Robyn was getting tired of the lectures. It had been an exhausting day and now, with her belly full, she just wanted to sleep. Luckily their mother seemed to know that. Paprika lay down and the cubs snuggled into her thick warm coat and were asleep within seconds.

CHAPTER THIRTEEN

Robyn opened her eyes to a world spinning out of control. She had a clear picture of Paprika's beautiful eyes locked onto hers. Then everything around her vibrated. She heard a loud eerie sound. Shivers ran along her spine. She didn't know where she was now. But she wasn't in the Arctic anymore. There was no bright white glare from the snow and ice. She was in a much darker place, and she felt a weightlessness as though perhaps she was suspended. "Whoomp. Whoomp," came the eerie sound again. Robyn sensed the presence of something huge right beside her. She was almost too scared to turn her head to look. Then she heard Paprika's voice. "It's okay Robyn, it's only me."

Robyn forced herself to calm down. Gingerly, she turned her head. Robyn wasn't sure what form Paprika would take this time, but she was starting to get used to this craziness. Or so she thought – she definitely wasn't expecting this. Right beside her was the biggest creature she'd ever seen. There was a massive whale close to her. Even the word 'massive' was an understatement, as this creature was gigantic. She'd seen pictures and movies of blue whales, but nothing could have prepared her for this. "Oh my goodness, Pappi, you are gigantanormous!"

Paprika laughed and went into lecture mode. "Blue whales can weigh as much as forty elephants do," Paprika explained. "Follow me. Let's see what life is like when you are one of the biggest creatures on Earth." And with that, she rose smoothly to the surface of the water. She exhaled through her huge blowhole, sending up a vapour cloud metres into the air. She took in the fresh air and then glided back into the ocean. Her tail flukes hardly made a splash as they re-entered the surface. Then her streamlined body quickly cut through the water as she plummeted to the ocean depths. For such a huge creature, she was wonderfully elegant.

Robyn copied Paprika's movements as they headed towards some deep underwater canyons. Although Robyn was colossal, she felt gentle, sleek and incredibly beautiful. Her tail was large and powerful. It took minimal effort to propel herself swiftly downwards. The ocean seemed to part like silky curtains as Robyn's enormous body glided through. The dark, watery environment was comfortable and relaxing. "Where's Brad?" Robyn asked as she looked around for her brother, expecting to see him in the form of a whale.

"He's not with us now. He's snug and warm in his bed at home. Look at all the krill, Robyn. Just what I was hoping for. Watch and copy what I do," Paprika said. Robyn quickly did as instructed and lunged forward with her immense jaws wide open. Robyn gulped in thousands of litres of water and krill. As she pressed her tongue against the baleen plates in her mouth the water shot back out leaving the krill behind, which she swallowed greedily. The tiny shrimp-like morsels tasted delicious.

"That's so cool, it's so easy," said Robyn with amazement at how simple it was for them to feed. After several minutes they rose back to the surface of the Indian Ocean. They gulped in another breath of air and descended once more to continue gorging themselves.

"We need millions of krill each day to sustain these

huge bodies," said Paprika. "So don't be shy."

Robyn wasn't shy as she gulped krill as fast as she could. Then she turned to Paprika and spat out krill and water together, almost choking in disgust at what she saw. "Ooh, that's revolting, Paprika," Robyn shouted. Paprika had pooped out a huge mass of orange gunk.

Paprika laughed. "Aren't you glad I don't poop like that when I'm your dog?" Without waiting for a reply, she thrust herself back to the surface. "Let's do some surface cruising," she suggested.

Robyn shouted after Paprika, "Sounds like a good idea. I've just lost my appetite, thanks to you."

They slid in and out of the water's surface in a soothing rhythm, blowing columns of spray high into the air. As their tails lifted above the surface, water streamed off their flukes like waterfalls. "Okay, now let's have some fun," Paprika said, as she catapulted herself up and out of the water. She turned in mid-air and thumped back down with a tremendous splash.

Robyn copied her, laughing in delight. "That feels so good. Like a back scratch."

As they prepared for the next breach, Robyn noticed a large boat heading their way. Paprika was already reacting. She shouted, "Robyn dive as deep as you can and get as far away from here as possible. It's a renegade whaler and they are out to kill us. Swim fast and don't stop. I will find you later."

"I can't leave you alone. You'll be in danger."

"Go, Robyn. I have a better chance of escape on my own. If I'm worrying about you, I won't be able to figure out what to do, and they will have two targets, instead of one. Go! Now!"

Robyn understood Paprika's reasoning, but she froze. She couldn't bring herself to dive and leave her friend in trouble. But she didn't know how to help. So she moved away but stayed close enough to make sure Paprika was okay. Just then a harpoon flew through the air towards

Paprika, who seemed unaware that they were already close enough to fire. The spear's shaft glanced off Paprika's side, and immediately she dived. But it took time for her body to be totally submerged. Just as the water was closing over her tail, a second harpoon flew. Robyn heard a thump as it hit Paprika. It penetrated the tip of her right fluke. Paprika's body jerked and her descent slowed. She writhed in apparent agony and moaned in desperation. She thrashed her tail. She spun her body as much as the connecting harpoon allowed. But the pressure against her tail must have been increasing. Robyn could tell that Paprika was in a bad way as she pulled the boat, with the barb embedded in her flesh. The water vibrated with signals of pain and distress. She was calling out for help.

Robyn was frantic. She didn't know what to do about this unexpected crisis. She was appalled by her uselessness. Then she heard a deafening sound. It was getting closer. She thought it must be the propellers of the boat. Then a deep booming voice said, "Rika, hold on, I'm coming." Another blue whale was racing towards her friend. This one was even larger than Paprika.

"Levi, help me," shrieked Paprika.

"Rika, I'm going to save you. It's going to hurt, so be brave. Keep pulling as hard as you can," Levi said in a deep, calm voice. He propelled himself towards the boat at high speed. As he neared the vessel, he raised his body to the surface and bashed into it with astonishing force. Robyn could feel shock waves pulsate around her.

Paprika screamed in pain. The harpoon ripped away from her flesh. The ocean around her turned red. There was splashing and screaming from around the boat, which was somehow still afloat. Two men had fallen into the water. Levi was close and the men cried in terror. Other men on board shouted for their fellow hunters to get back on the boat. Another man fumbled to load a new harpoon into the gun.

"Rika, dive!" commanded Levi as he made another

dash towards the boat. Paprika dived immediately. Robyn followed without hesitation. She turned back in time to see Levi strike the boat again. His back collided with incredible force. Most of the boat disappeared from Robyn's view as it became airborne. Then it crashed back down through the surface of the water, upside down. Men screamed as they landed in the water near Levi. He ignored them.

"Okay Rika, you are safe now. I'm not going to hurt those men. I just hope they will never go whale hunting again." Without another glance at the terrified men, Levi swam to Paprika to comfort her and check her wound. She was in shock and disoriented, swimming in large circles, with a trail of blood creating ribbons of red through the water. "Thank goodness the harpoon was in your fluke and not buried in your body," said Levi.

Robyn made her way to Paprika, rubbing against her side to show her concern and care. Levi touched Rika's bleeding fluke. Robyn watched wide-eyed as the tear healed miraculously in front of her eyes. Levi laughed, a long low rumble which vibrated the water all around them. He said with a chuckle, "Now you won't even have a scar to tell the tale. Excuse the pun."

"Thank you Levi for saving my life and for healing my injury," replied Paprika. "You are wonderful for coming to my rescue. Now I think I should get Robyn home. She's had enough excitement for one day."

"It is my job and my pleasure to look after you Rika. We will meet again soon. I look forward to seeing you again too, Robyn."

Paprika touched Levi's jaw with hers and then turned back to Robyn with a sparkle in her eye. Robyn was confused. What did he mean about meeting again? She said, "What... ."

Robyn's world spun out of control. She was falling and spinning, faster and faster and faster... .

CHAPTER FOURTEEN

Robyn's body jerked awake. She groaned and rolled over, thankful it was Saturday. Yay, no school today. An extra half-hour in bed, she thought as she dozed off to sleep again. But that wasn't to be, as a soft furry face touched her cheek and a long tongue licked her nose. She opened her eyes to Paprika staring at her, willing her to get up. Robyn smiled and lazily stroked her dog as she groaned and closed her eyes again. That was wishful thinking. Paprika made a short, sharp noise that sounded like 'Oof'. That meant she wanted to go outside. Robyn dragged herself out of bed with a sigh. That was the end of her sleep-in. Paprika licked Robyn's hand and then ran to the bedroom door in anticipation.

Brad accosted Robyn the moment she appeared downstairs. "Robyn, I had such an amazing dream last night, and I can remember it."

"Yeah, big deal. And so?"

The words tumbled out of Brad so fast that Robyn could hardly make sense of them. "You and I were in the Arctic. We were polar bear cubs. We were with Paprika. She was a bear too. Our mother. She was teaching us to hunt seals. Yuk, I ate seal. So did you."

"Oh, wow. My dog was a polar bear? What a weird messed-up dream. Why are you so excited? Because I was with you, I suppose?" teased Robyn.

"Yeah, right. Love having my big sister telling me what to do. Hah, I told you not to tell me what to do. Because I was the same age as you. So there."

"Cool. Glad you got to tell me off. Maybe you should go online to find out what your dream means. It doesn't mean anything to me. Only that you'd like to be my big brother. I'm going running now."

Robyn felt tired this morning, like she sometimes did after a long swimming-training session. She hoped that a run might get her going. As she was running, she started thinking about her conversation with Brad. Maybe she should've been more interested in his dream. His excitement was evident. Maybe she'd check in with him when she got home. Maybe she'd be a good big sister and actually listen to him.

Paprika was setting a fast pace today, looking back at Robyn as she strained against her lead. Robyn wondered if it was herself being sluggish, or was the dog being more energetic than usual? Paprika seemed to be on top form today. Robyn said between breaths, "Hey Pappi, what's up with you today? Wish you could pass on some of that energy to me. Slow down." Paprika looked up at her and twitched her ears as though she understood. She slowed her pace. "Good girl." Robyn immediately felt better. By the time she got home she was re-energised. She laughed at the silly thought that popped into her head. It was almost as though Paprika really had passed some energy to her.

"Hey Brad, where are you?" Robyn called out once she had fed Paprika.

"In my room," shouted Brad.

"Can I come up and talk to you?"

"Yip," Brad replied.

Robyn entered his bedroom, with Paprika at her heels.

She apologised to Brad. "Sorry I was grumpy earlier. I was tired. But your dream sounds interesting. Do you want to tell me more about it?"

"Sure. It's weird, because I don't normally remember dreams, but this one's real cool. It's like a movie in my head," Brad explained enthusiastically, as he recounted his dream in detail to Robyn. As he began talking, she understood his excitement. She could somehow feel the cold ice. She could sense the crispness of the Arctic air, the size of the mother bear and the warm comfort of her thick coat. Even the idea of eating a seal, for some reason didn't disgust her. Robyn appeared to be 'feeling' Brad's story. It reminded her of the essay she wrote about the penguins.

"Wow, Brad, you are becoming a good storyteller. It's like I can feel what the cubs felt," Robyn said to Brad.

"Really? That's awesome. Maybe I should write it down before I forget it?" Brad replied.

"Good idea. Thanks for sharing with me. No wonder you were excited. You remembered your dream explicitly. Wish I could remember my dreams. I don't remember anything. Sometimes I get a fleeting glimpse of a dream when I wake, but it's gone before I can properly capture it," Robyn said with a sigh. "Anyway, see you later. I've got to make a pizza to take to Hayley's tonight. We're having a sleepover for her birthday."

"Okay, bye."

Robyn felt better that she'd paid her little brother attention. Too often she ignored him, or just found him annoying. She should try harder to be a good sister to him.

Paprika charged downstairs with Robyn, barking and running around the coffee table. "No Paprika, no time to play. You're supposed to be tired after the run."

After preparing the pizza, Robyn pulled the vacuum cleaner out of the cupboard. Paprika rushed to her safe place behind the armchair. "Paprika, you're such a wuss. Just like Dad – scared of the vacuum cleaner," Robyn laughed at her lame joke. But it wasn't far from the truth.

Her dad never vacuumed. "It's because of all the hair you shed that I have to get the monster out of the cupboard so often. Oh well, at least you'll get some rest now." Robyn put her headphones on and selected an energetic playlist on her cell phone. She strapped the phone onto her upper arm and connected it to the headphones. Now vacuuming would be much less of an effort. She would dance her way around the house.

CHAPTER FIFTEEN

In the mid-afternoon, Robyn's mum dropped off her and Paprika at the local dog-training club for agility practice. "I'll see you in about an hour," Carol said.

"Okay, thanks Mum," said Robyn as Paprika pulled excitedly on her lead. "No pulling, Paprika. Sit. Good girl, now heel." Paprika was excited. It was evident to Robyn that she was trying to contain herself though, as she tried to stop pulling. Robyn loved Saturday afternoons at the dog club. There was absolutely no doubt that Paprika did too. They had only been able to start a few months ago as they couldn't start until Paprika's bones and growth plates had developed properly. Now they were getting right into it. It was a shame that they'd had so much rain over the last few months. There had been no training for a couple of weeks as the ground had been too wet and dangerous for practice.

"Hi Dan, how are you? Is the ground okay again?"

"Hi, Robyn. It doesn't seem too boggy. Hopefully, the weather will settle now that spring is over. We need to practise every week. Hi Pappi, how are you, girl?" Dan said, as Paprika jumped up at him in her excitement.

"Off, Paprika. Sit. Good girl. Now say hello." Robyn

took Paprika through the usual drill. Paprika liked Dan and was always so happy to see him that she couldn't seem to resist jumping up at him.

"I don't mind, Robyn. Though of course, you're right to stop her jumping up," Dan said. He knelt down and gave Paprika rubs all over her head and body. "Hey girl, I missed you."

Robyn hitched Paprika's lead over one of the hooks on the clubhouse wall. Then she helped set up the agility equipment on the field. The fun began!

Some of the dogs were fast, others slow and precise, and some of them totally nuts – like Jasper, who did the first two jumps and the first tunnel. Then he was off, charging across the grass to play with the dogs jumping in the beginners' class. His trainer called him back. He only came half-way and then bolted back to the much more interesting young terrier across the field.

As Robyn watched Jasper race across towards the beginners' class, she saw the back of a somehow familiar male figure. Sitting quietly next to him was a large german shepherd. The boy turned towards her. Their eyes met in recognition, and Ryan waved at her. Robyn's heart skipped a beat as she waved back. She quickly focused back on their course as she felt her face flush. How embarrassing!

Jock, the huntaway, was crazy – hit one, miss one, jump one, skid through one. Oh, well done. One correct. Through the tunnel at breakneck speed. All while barking nonstop. Jock's owner laughed, enjoying this for the fun factor. Paprika joined in with the barking whenever Jock was on the course, and she pulled at her restraint. She got very excited as he rushed around telling the world what fun it was.

Dan's dog, Dash, was next. She was a black-and-white border collie and aptly named, as she moved at high speed. Dan had trained her well. He didn't have to keep up with her as his body language and hand signals were precise. She understood from a distance what he wanted. Added to that, she was incredibly nimble with the twists and turns. They were hard to match – no wonder they'd won some championships. Robyn would definitely need to take tips from them.

Robyn loved watching all the dogs. Each had its particular temperament and amusing ways.

As Robyn lifted the lead from the hook, she said, "Okay Pappi, your turn – finally." And with that Paprika yanked Robyn towards the course. At the start, Robyn unclipped the lead and held onto Paprika's collar. "Down. Wait," she commanded as she walked away. She wanted to get past the start and to the right of the first jump or two as Dan had instructed. But Paprika had other ideas and whipped around the first jump to get to Robyn. "No Paprika, I said stay," Robyn gently chided as she led her over-eager young dog back to the start. She gave her the 'down and wait' command again. This time, as Robyn walked away, she put her hand up in the 'stop' sign and kept repeating, "Wait." When she was almost level with the second jump, she shouted back to Paprika, "Go! Jump!"

Paprika had read Robyn's body language, and was already in the air over the first jump before Robyn got the 'go' command out. Robyn ran as fast as she could. She extended her arm and pointed towards the obstacles that she wanted Paprika to tackle. Paprika was so quick that Robyn battled to shout the commands fast enough. Dan was always telling her to give the next command when she was on the previous obstacle. But it was hard to get it right when there was so much to consider. She did her best and yelled, "Jump, tunnel, right, walk on – slow, slow, jump, left – no not that jump." Too late, Paprika was already over the wrong jump. And she was looking to Robyn for the next command. Robyn realised her mistake and spun quickly, calling Paprika towards the blue tunnel. As she turned she slipped on the moist grass, falling on her butt. Paprika was on top of her like a shot, licking her face and then bounding around, licking again and yapping at her as though telling her to get up. How embarrassing!

Dan laughed and shouted, "Paprika's asking what you're doing down there. You're supposed to be running. No time to rest. Get up!" The other trainers all laughed with Dan, and Robyn felt her face flush again. "Are you okay, Robyn?" As she nodded, he added, "We all have hiccups and fall sometimes. I suggest you get some studded shoes to stop you slipping. The ground's still quite wet and slippery. Even when it's dry you can slip, especially when you have a fast dog like Paprika. I've landed on my arse many times."

Robyn got up, with Paprika leaping around her ready to get going again.

"Take it from the jump after the dog walk again, and try to get her attention before she does that second jump. It's meant to trick you. That one is right in the dog's line of sight and flows from the previous obstacle, so you have to get her attention fast."

Robyn called Paprika to a spot just after the dog walk. She positioned Paprika on her right side so that she could turn to the left immediately after the jump. "Jump! Left!" Robyn yelled, as she ducked to her left towards the blue tunnel. She was careful not to confuse Paprika with the weave poles. This time, Paprika got the message in time and whipped around to the left as she came out of the jump. Robyn was already shouting, "Tunnel." Paprika dived into it without question, and Robyn yelled, "Jump – right – A-frame – slow." She didn't want her to hurtle down and miss the coloured contact section at the bottom of the frame.

Paprika slowed and touched the contact, but Robyn wasn't quick enough with the next command. Paprika dashed back to the two jumps and the red tunnel. She completely missed the row of obstacles in the centre of the course that should have been next. Robyn called her back and sent Paprika over the centre two jumps. Then in a straight line over the dog walk. "Yay, good girl," she said in an excited tone of voice. She wanted to let Paprika know that she'd done well and that she was happy with her. Paprika leapt around Robyn in joy. Robyn clapped her hands twice and Paprika propelled herself into Robyn's arms. Robyn caught her with one arm under the tail and the other supporting her back. Paprika looked proudly over Robyn's shoulder. The other trainers laughed and clapped.

"Well done girls. Mistakes, as always, were trainer error, but you are getting better, and that's one super-fast dog. Get it right, Robyn, and you might be competing against Dash and me in the future."

Robyn was elated to hear that, although she'd made mistakes, they were improving. They were doing well as a team. And to hear that Paprika had potential was great news. She'd have to ask Dad to make some jumps and weave poles for them to practise at home. Training once a week wouldn't get them to competition level.

After a few more rounds, the training session came to an end.

Robyn gave Paprika water and looped her lead over the wall hook. Then she helped put the equipment back into the storeroom.

"Thanks Dan, see you next week," Robyn said as Dan bent down to stroke Paprika.

"Bye Robyn. Bye Paprika. Don't forget to practise the wait command."

Robyn and Paprika walked across the field to the parking area to wait for Robyn's mum to arrive. As they were waiting, Ryan and his dog walked over towards them. "Hey Robyn, that was fantastic. I saw you two crazies rush around that course – you were awesome."

"Thanks, Ryan – it's such fun, even though I fell on my butt! Paprika's doing so well. I make all the mistakes and mess up by confusing her or not giving her instructions in time. I haven't seen you here before. When did you start?"

"It was our first time today. We were supposed to start last weekend, but I had a gynmastics competition. This is Max. Hi Paprika," he said as he bent down to stroke Paprika's ears.

"Hello, Max. You're a big boy, aren't you?" Robyn said as she placed her hand in front of Max's nose for him to sniff and accept her. "How old is he, Ryan?"

"He's just over three. I should have started this a while ago but was concentrating on the obedience first. A big dog like him can appear quite intimidating, so I wanted to be sure that he would show respect and be calm and friendly, and non-aggressive."

"Looks like you've done a good job. He's gorgeous and very approachable. Even Paprika likes him and, quite honestly, she can sometimes be a right little bitch with other dogs. If she's scared or if they get in her face when she hasn't initiated it, she can be snappy. But look at her – I swear she's flirting with him." Robyn had never seen Paprika react like that to another dog. Robyn laughed as Paprika sidled up to Max, rolled over and then acted coy. "Oh my goodness, next she's going to flutter her eyelashes like... ." Robyn stopped in mid-sentence. She couldn't believe that she nearly said, 'like Gina.' And to say that to Ryan of all people. Robyn felt heat sear her cheeks. She quickly bent over to make a fuss of Max, hoping to hide her embarrassment. Max wasn't interested in Robyn now. His attention was on Paprika as he gently sniffed and nudged her with his nose.

Ryan laughed. "Her flirting is working. I wonder where she learned to do that."

Robyn jerked her head up to deny that Paprika learned it from her as Ryan seemed to be suggesting. As she did, Ryan started laughing. Robyn immediately relaxed and was able to compose herself. She even managed to reply in the same light tone, "Not from me, that's for sure."

Ryan totally surprised Robyn as he asked, "Maybe she's met Gina?" and winked at Robyn.

"Yeah, you'd think so. But Paprika definitely hasn't met Gina," Robyn replied. "Gina and I aren't exactly friends."

"I've noticed, and I'm not surprised. I hope you didn't think I was rude on the bus when Gina butted in between us when we were talking? I felt like a right idiot about it."

Robyn couldn't believe what she was hearing. Guys weren't sensitive to people's feelings like this, were they? Had she finally met a teenage boy who was sincere and caring, who wasn't just thinking with his hormones?

"Uh, no," Robyn stammered. "No, you weren't rude. It's Gina – she hates me."

"Why would she hate you? I think she's just like that with all girls."

"Well, she's not exactly friendly to most girls, but she's downright nasty to me. But it doesn't matter," Robyn added unconvincingly. She was feeling uncomfortable with this turn of conversation. She'd never spoken to a guy about this sort of thing before and it felt weird. Luckily, at that moment Paprika leapt up and barked excitedly. She'd seen their car pulling into the car park. "There's my mum," Robyn said, letting out a quiet sigh of relief.

"Well, it was great to see you Robyn, and to meet your little flirt, Paprika," Ryan said with a grin.

Something in Ryan's attitude put Robyn at ease again. She said, "Yeah it was good to see you and I'm glad that you and that lovely big boy of yours have joined agility. Bye, see you at school."

"Sure, see you soon. Enjoy your weekend. Bye Paprika."

Paprika jumped into the back of the car. Robyn told her mum that Paprika had done well and about Dan's comment. "We'll have to get Dad to help with some jump building," Carol suggested to Robyn.

"I was going to ask about that. Maybe Dad can make me some poles with sharp ends so that we can stick them in the ground for weave practice?" Robyn asked.

"I'm sure he can work something out for you."

When they got home, Paprika drank loads of water and lay down contentedly. Robyn was thrilled that she had found an exercise both she and Paprika loved. And having Ryan there now was an added bonus, even if she did seem to do dumb things whenever he was around.

CHAPTER SIXTEEN

Robyn wrapped up a candle that she had made for Hayley. She separately wrapped a gorgeous bright-blue top that would look lovely with Hayley's dark hair and blue eyes. She was pleased that she had saved money from her dog-walking stints over the school holidays to buy Hayley's gift. It felt good to have earned her own money and to spend some of it on her best friend.

It should be a pretty chilled evening at Hayley's. Their school friend Sarah, and Hayley's life-long friend Megan, would be there.

Robyn arrived early at Hayley's house. She wanted to tell Hayley what had happened at school while she was away. She hadn't wanted to discuss it over the phone. Hayley's mum opened the door to Robyn and embraced her in a big hug. "Hi Jody, how are you?" Robyn asked, as she was released and could breathe again.

"Great thanks, Robyn, especially after our cruise - it was amazing. I can see you are good – you look fit and gorgeous," she replied with a grin.

Robyn felt the colour rush to her cheeks for the umpteenth time that day. She said politely, "I'm well, thanks. Trying to keep up with Paprika keeps me fit."

"That's good. I haven't seen her for a while, but she was a beautiful puppy. You should bring her around to visit sometime. You know I love dogs, and if she's well behaved, she's welcome inside the house. She can certainly go downstairs."

"Thanks Jody, I'll bring her to see you soon."

"Hayley's getting the room ready downstairs. I'll take the pizza to the kitchen for you. You go on down."

"Thanks," said Robyn as she handed the pizza to Hayley's mum.

"Robyn I'm down here," shouted Hayley at the sound of Robyn's voice.

"Yip, on my way," Robyn called back as she hurried down the stairs and gave her best friend a hug and handed over the gifts. "Happy Birthday! Wow, the room looks great Hayley."

"Thanks – I'll open these when the others get here. I'm so lucky as Mum and Dad are letting me have the room exclusively now, since they redecorated it. It's my birthday gift from them," Hayley said with obvious delight.

"Wow, it's awesome. Great birthday present – you are so lucky to have a space like this. My bedroom just doesn't work as an entertainment space for friends. As you know Mum gets upset with me because I don't ask friends around often enough. But there's nowhere in my house to entertain," Robyn said as she appraised the room.

There was a big TV with sound system, hooked up and ready to go. Two chocolate-brown sleeper-couches and a sturdy old coffee table stood on a large cream rug. In the corner of the wooden flooring was a heap of scatter cushions. A small fridge hummed away in the corner. The room was separated from the rest of the house by a door near the staircase.

"We can move the rug and coffee table out the way if we want to dance," Hayley said with a grin. "Dad also did up the bathroom as it was gross. Come have a look."

"Looks amazing – all bright and clean," Robyn

remarked.

"And I have to keep it that way. A price worth paying to have this space. Come look at this... ." Hayley opened the blinds in front of sliding doors. There was a beautiful little deck area outside. It was about three metres square. At the back was a retaining wall and bed full of colourful leafy plants. "Dad's promised to look after the plants, as he knows I can't keep anything alive."

"Wow, it looks great."

"That area was such a mess before. It was full of moss and weeds. Dad got me to pull all the weeds out this morning. Then I water-blasted it while he went out and bought soil and plants. I can't believe how fast it all came together. Dad will put a table and a couple of chairs out there, and may put a little awning over it."

"It's amazing – lucky you," Robyn said as she gave Hayley a big grin.

"Hayley, I don't want to spoil your birthday, but I have to tell you what happened while you were away. It's been the worst few days of my life."

"Oh no, Robyn. Why didn't you say something before?"

"I didn't want to tell you over the phone and I obviously couldn't tell you at school. It was all horrible." Hayley hugged Robyn and gently pushed her onto the couch and sat next to her, waiting for Robyn to continue.

"On Sunday when you left I sent you a text saying, 'Maybe Gina wants to be my bf while you're away, lol.' I added a smiley face and a wink at the end, so it was obviously a joke. The only problem was, I sent the text to Hayley Connor by mistake. She told Gina and, by the time I got to school on Monday, everyone was either ignoring me or hating on me. I had no idea what was going on. It was so upsetting. One day I had friends and the next day no-one was talking to me. I finally found out that a rumour had gone around about the text. Gina had totally turned it around and told people that I'd said awful things about her and called her all sorts of disgusting names. Things I would never say. I couldn't believe that my dumb joke had caused such hatred towards me.

"It was as though the whole school thought I was the biggest bitch on the planet. I was devastated. Even Sarah didn't stand by me. She phoned me in the evening and apologised. But she still didn't support me at school. She's such a softie. She said that she was scared to stand with me against the bullies. I understand and don't blame her. But I felt so alone. Nobody talked to me. I'd been rejected by everyone. And it was so unfair as Gina had blown it all out of proportion. From my silly comment, that was meant to be a joke, I ended up being banished by everyone.

"I was so humiliated. I couldn't look anyone in the eye. I looked down when I walked through the school corridors and avoided all the places we normally went. I was paranoid. I thought everyone was watching me and laughing at me and bad-mouthing me all the time. I wanted to cry constantly. I've felt so alone. I didn't even want to tell my mum. Luckily, I had Paprika to talk to. She may not know what I'm saying, but she makes me feel better. It's bad enough that Gina hates me, but I can't deal with everyone else hating me and judging me wrongly. Oh, Hayley, it's all been so hard." Robyn could barely get the last words out between sobs. Tears streaked mascara down her face.

Hayley grabbed a handful of tissues from the table and wiped the streaks off Robyn's face. She handed the tissues to her friend. "Oh Robyn, I'm sorry I wasn't there for you. But I'm back now, and I've got your back. You are going to walk tall and proud. You've done nothing wrong, and we are going to set the record straight. I'm sure Gina's just jealous of you. You are so gorgeous and everyone loves you."

"Sarah's here, Hayley," Jody called down the stairs.

"Coming Mum," Hayley shouted back to her mum. "Robyn, take a deep breath and try to relax," she said and rushed upstairs to greet her friend.

Robyn went into the bathroom to splash water on her face. As she opened the bathroom door she heard Hayley saying, "What were you thinking, taking sides with Gina over Robyn? Have you gone crazy?"

Robyn was horrified. She didn't expect Hayley to confront Sarah about it at the birthday party. She shouldn't have said anything to Hayley.

As Robyn emerged from the bathroom, Sarah seemed to shrink into herself. "I'm so sorry. I feel so bad. I don't understand the power Gina has over people, especially me. She really scares me. I didn't know how to stand up to her and just seemed to get pulled along with all of them. I'm so pathetic. And I feel sick about what I did. Or rather what I didn't do. I didn't stand beside my friend. There's no excuse, I know. I don't deserve friends like you. I wanted to tell everyone that Gina was telling lies. But I just couldn't do it. Robyn, please forgive me."

Robyn replied, "Maybe I would have done the same in your position. I understand, Sarah, but please come back to me. We need to stick together. And now that Hayley's back, we'll all be stronger."

Hayley put her arms around her friends. "We're survivors, okay?"

The three girls hugged and agreed to support each other against all odds.

The doorbell rang. Robyn was relieved that Megan hadn't been there when Hayley had tackled Sarah. That would have been so embarrassing.

Hayley welcomed Megan into the group as though nothing had happened. Sarah and Robyn looked at each other and smiled. Robyn squeezed Sarah's hand to let her know she was forgiven.

The friends sang 'Happy Birthday' to Hayley. Then she opened her gifts. "Oh, Robyn thank you, this candle will be perfect on the coffee table. And I love, love, love this top... hope I can get it over these big boobs of mine," she joked, as usual, about her small breasts. "It's beautiful, thanks."

Sarah had given her a pair of sunglasses. She knew the style that Hayley liked and that she had recently broken her old ones. "You're a lifesaver Sarah – just what I needed, thanks."

Megan's gift was quite big and solid. "Any guesses, Hayley?" Megan asked before Hayley ripped the paper open.

"No idea. You know I don't like suspense. I'm just going to open it and see." With that Hayley tore the paper from end to end, exposing a wooden box containing a dartboard.

"Love it, thanks. It's the perfect addition to my new area. Let's have dinner, then we can play some games," Hayley said as she led the way back upstairs.

They enjoyed their meal, ate too much, and decided to dance before settling down for a game. Robyn and Hayley moved the table and rug to one side and Hayley cranked up the dance music. They opened the doors to the deck to let in some fresh air while they danced until they were all exhausted.

"That was such fun to dance. We should do that more often – it makes me feel so alive," Hayley grinned.

"Yeah, it's such good exercise. I'm so unfit," Sarah added.

Hayley dropped the volume, closed the door, and they pushed the furniture back into place. Sitting on cushions around the table, they opted for a game of 'Celebrities', which caused much laughter.

Once the second game finished they were all starting to fade. "Thanks everyone for making my birthday so special," Hayley said. "It's been such fun. Let's get the beds sorted." They moved the table out of the way and pulled out the sleeper couches, pushing them together so there'd be plenty of room for the four of them to sleep comfortably.

Robyn was exhausted after her busy and emotional day, and fell asleep within seconds of her head hitting her pillow.

CHAPTER SEVENTEEN

Robyn was exhilarated. She had longed to do this since she was a little girl – to fly like a bird – now here she was soaring above the treetops with ease, feeling the rush of air against her feathers. She looked at her outstretched wings in wonder as she inhaled the heady scents of the jungle below.

"How do you feel, Robyn?" Paprika asked as she flew over Robyn's head and glided gracefully in front of her.

"Unbelievable." Robyn squealed in delight as she tipped her right wing and veered off to the right of Paprika. Robyn lifted her wing again and steadied, then flung herself to the left. With head down and feathers furled, she then dive-bombed towards the trees below, letting out a shrill squawk as she gained speed and hurtled towards the tree canopy. Then she lifted her head and dropped her tail and feet, extending her wings. This combination slowed her down as she neared her target. She stretched her legs and opened her claws, grasping for her selected perch. With a feeling of great achievement, she landed gently and right on target. Paprika flew past her and Robyn had a chance to appreciate her beauty and elegance. The undersides of Paprika's wings were gold.

There was a band of bright turquoise-blue where the topside feathers met those underneath her body. Robyn could clearly see smaller gold feathers above the long flight-feathers. The primary wing-tip quills spread out as Paprika glided overhead. As she banked and turned, Robyn saw how the plumage on Paprika's back glistened. Green framed her white face with its distinctive black markings. Her beak was huge and almost black, and she had a magnificent long tail. The only things not quite in harmony with this beautiful macaw were the eyes, which were amber dog-eyes. Paprika expertly landed on the same branch as Robyn and rubbed her head against Robyn's wing.

"Hey Robyn, please will you give my neck a quick preen? I have a new feather coming through and that shaft won't budge. It's so annoying."

"Haha – grooming you again. As a dog, you don't like being brushed," Robyn said as she gently pulled the shaft off the new feather.

"Well, that's because you're so rough."

"I try to be gentle, but I have to pull to get all those knots out of your fur. And if you'd sit still, I may find it easier."

"Fair enough. I don't like having knots in my coat, and I always feel good once the tugging is over. So, I forgive you for giving me the rough treatment," Paprika replied as, with a twinkle in her eye, she yanked a little feather out of Robyn's chest.

"Ouch! What was that for?"

"Sorry, I thought I saw a knot in your feather," Paprika said with a squawk.

"Touché," Robyn laughed. "So, what's the story? I'd love to know what's going on."

"Well, we are macaws, in the Amazon jungle. And we're about to look for some tasty seeds to eat," Paprika responded.

"I kind of gathered that, Pappi. What I meant was,

what are these dreams about? They're pretty confusing."

"I know. Remember I told you, when we were penguins, to just enjoy yourself? Well, I guess you've now experienced enough that I can tell you a little more about these excursions we have been going on."

"Okay, how about this for starters. Why can I remember everything when we are in these dreams, but when I wake up I can't remember anything?" Robyn blurted out with words tripping over each other in her haste. She took a deep breath and continued more slowly as she tried to get her thoughts in order. "Right now I can recall being a penguin and almost being eaten by a seal. Tobogganing on the ice, meeting Gwen, and later waking up in my bed as me, the human. Everything that's happened since, as human, polar bear, and whale, is crystal clear now. But I have a feeling that when I wake from this, it will all be forgotten. And I didn't dream like this last night at Hayley's."

"I wasn't with you at Hayley's. And you are correct – you won't remember these dreams when you are awake. Your conscious mind wouldn't be able to understand. But the feelings and experiences should remain with you at a deep subconscious level. You will now have an innate understanding of the things that you have experienced and seen in these dreams. You won't have to question how or why, you will just accept. For example, when you wrote the essay about penguins, you knew how it felt to dive down deep into the water and how clear the Antarctic Ocean was. You knew because you retained that experience in your subconscious mind. These dreams are like real experiences, as the knowledge and sensations remain within your subconscious, even though you won't remember the actual dream. I know it's hard to grasp this concept, but with time you will learn to trust your judgement and inner awareness," Paprika explained.

"Wow," Robyn exclaimed. "No wonder I don't remember. Can you imagine if I told my friends that I had been a penguin? Or a polar bear, or a blue whale, or a parrot? With my dog, who could talk to me in English! They would think I've gone bonkers. I think I've gone bonkers. But at least it explains why I was able to write so quickly about penguins for my essay. And I figured I was suddenly getting smarter."

"Of course you are getting smarter. And you are learning a lot about yourself and your world."

"What exactly is it all about then?" asked Robyn.

"I can't tell you too much now, Robyn."

"But I have so many questions, and there are so many things that I need to know. Like who or what are you?" Robyn insisted.

"Just know that I am your friend in whatever form I appear in these dreams, and you can trust me implicitly. Though during your waking hours, I am just a dog. A really super-smart one."

Robyn nodded.

"By getting small amounts of information at a time, it will be easier to comprehend. It will become clearer. You will have some amazing experiences during this process," Paprika added. "It's going to take a while even for your subconscious mind to accept all this. Just know that you are very special. You have been selected to assist with a critical task. But there's a lot to see and learn before we can be sure that you are ready for this incredible challenge."

"How come Brad remembered the dream with the polar bears? I couldn't remember anything?"

"Brad's not part of the mission, so it's safe for him to remember his experience as a dream. It was also an experiment to see how you would respond to his recollection. The experiment was a success. Initially, you didn't want to give your brother any of your time. That's a pretty typical sibling response. But you pondered about it. You realised that you had been unfair and snappy with him. Later you invited him to tell you his story, which was a mature and unselfish thing to do. And then you responded with feeling and understanding as he recounted his dream. It proved that all is well with the process and selection choice. Although you cannot be allowed to remember the dreams, you need to align with the experience. You will learn to respect and follow your gut instinct or intuition. If you had remembered that as a dream, like Brad did, then we would not be able to continue this process," Paprika explained.

"Why? And what process?"

"At this stage, I can only let you know that you are not alone. Many other young people around the world are going through a similar process."

"It's great to know that I will have company somewhere out there during this process. But I don't understand." Robyn flapped her wings in frustration.

"I know, but for now let's discover this incredible and immense Amazon rainforest. Best to fuel up before we go. There are some tasty seeds on that tree over there." Paprika took off and landed on the branch of a tree with long, hanging seed pods, deftly cracking one open.

Robyn followed Paprika's lead. She had a delightful feast of seeds and fruit. Robyn ate until she was so full she was concerned she might not be able to take off again. But it was no problem. Her strong wings lifted her with ease as she followed her friend. They arrived in an area where there were hundreds of macaws. They were hanging onto a clay river bank and nibbling away at it. "Why do they do that?" Robyn asked.

"Some of the seeds and fruits are toxic. The sodium in the clay-licks helps neutralise the toxins," Paprika explained.

"Wow, nature sure is amazing," Robyn said as she tentatively tested the soil with her beak and tongue. "Oh, I was expecting it to taste revolting. It's not bad." The other birds chatted noisily as they gorged themselves on the sodium-rich clay. It was a sociable gathering. Robyn found the antics of the birds amusing as some of them quite obviously searched out a mate. One of the males was doing a dance. He dipped his head and pushed out his chest, trying to get a female's attention. She raised her beak in the air, totally ignoring him. He became more and more frustrated and persistent. Finally, she gave in by tucking her head into her chest, accepting his attention. Robyn got the feeling that the female hadn't entirely given in and the male would still have to work hard to win her over.

Some of the parrots flew off, squawking and screeching in a cacophony of sound. They must have had their fill of anti-toxins. As they left, others arrived to join the party.

The clash of sounds and colours left Robyn awestruck. What other amazing sights did the Amazon rainforest have in store for her, she wondered.

CHAPTER EIGHTEEN

Paprika and Robyn moved on to explore the river as it twisted and turned through lush vegetation. They stopped to watch the alligator-like caimans as they thrashed around in a synchronised ballet, rounding up their prey. The panicked fish had little chance of survival as different species worked in mutual interaction. If the fish escaped the caimans, black skimmers merely skimmed the fish into their open beaks as they flew over, or egrets waiting at the river's edge plucked them out of the water.

As Robyn and Paprika continued up the majestic Amazon River, Robyn saw two pink river-dolphins leaping in and out of the water in unison. She glimpsed an electric eel as it slid up to the surface for air. A school of the feared piranhas attacked a massive anaconda. The anaconda was coming off worse, as the razor teeth of the crazed piranhas ripped it to shreds.

"We're going to get into the thick of it now – literally," said Paprika as she changed course. She flew away from the river bank towards the dense jungle. Robyn followed Paprika over the profusion of bushes, vines and trees.

"I didn't realise just how immense this jungle would be – it appears to go on forever. And it's noisy. I can hear a myriad of insects as well as all the different calls from birds. It's amazing." Robyn was wide-eyed with wonder.

"It's the richest ecosystem in the world. But like everywhere else on Earth, it's being destroyed by man's interference. Although the Brazilian government has declared war on illegal loggers, it's such a vast area to protect. Daily, many square kilometres of forest are lost. Let's have a closer look at the activity down there," Paprika suggested. She dipped towards the trees in a graceful dive, coming to rest near the top of an enormous leafless tree, which must have been nearly two-hundred feet high. Robyn joined her on the lofty perch, towering above the other vegetation.

"This is one of the mighty kapok trees – incredible, isn't it?"

"It's gigantic. And it makes a great perch overlooking this spectacular view. But why is the tree bare?" Robyn asked.

"Being deciduous, they shed their leaves in the dry season," Paprika explained.

Robyn spotted an emperor tamarin watching them from the treetops below. He was such an unusual looking little fellow. His long white handlebar-moustache stuck out on either side of his face, curling around his pink nose and down towards his beard-like whiskers. The monkey's grey fur looked long and soft. He had big round dark eyes, and eyebrows that he appeared to be raising in surprise. As Robyn continued to study him, he lost interest in them. He continued his hunt for seeds. His long brown tail curled around a branch to steady him as his little black hands worked feverishly at the foliage.

"What a cutie," Robyn said. Just then she heard a strange loud noise. She followed the direction of the sound and realised that it came from a big monkey sitting in the treetop down to her left. It sounded like the creature had a sore throat as he howled, again and again, his mouth stretching wide with each roar.

"That's a howler monkey defending his turf. The sound carries for a few kilometres. And that incredibly long tail of his keeps him aloft in the tree tops," Paprika added.

"The howlers look pretty chilled though," Robyn noted. The family of reddish-brown primates casually picked leaves and fruit to eat. They didn't pay any attention to the birds watching them.

Robyn flew with Paprika over to a smaller tree. She glimpsed spider monkeys with their very long arms, legs and tails. The little grumpy-faced capuchin monkeys Robyn likened to little monks wearing brown robes with hoods. She spotted adorable tiny marmosets climbing along the branches after insects, and heard frog-calls from the jungle floor. And with her keen eyesight, she managed to spot a tarantula as it worked its way through the undergrowth. "I'm glad to be up here and not in the path of that scary looking spider," Robyn muttered.

"Shh, Robyn," Paprika whispered. "Look over there – about thirty metres to your right, then down quite low near that little clearing. There's a jaguar in the tree. It's pretty hard to see with its camouflaged colouring, but look carefully and keep quiet."

Robyn followed the direction of Paprika's line of sight. She couldn't see anything except branches, leaves and sun-filtered shadows. "I can't see it," Robyn whispered back.

"Keep your eyes pinned on that area just to the right of the clearing. It's in the tree with the almost horizontal branches, close to the forest floor."

Robyn focused on the spot that Paprika pointed out and still nothing. Then a slight flick of the jaguar's tail gave away its position to her keen eyes. "Got it," she whispered excitedly.

The two macaws stayed motionless for a couple of minutes. Their patience was rewarded as the jaguar crept down from its hiding place. It silently padded, step by stealthy step, towards a group of boar-like peccaries that seemed oblivious to the impending danger. The cat moved without a sound. It lifted and placed each foot with absolute precision, careful not to give away its presence by disturbing the leafy undergrowth. Robyn was awed by the spectacle and the beautiful rosette markings of the hunter. Nature's perfection and adaptation were incredible.

With its head held close to the ground and mouth slightly open, the jaguar crouched low to the ground. Its shoulder blades rhythmically lifted and fell as it moved stealthily towards the peccaries. Robyn could see its large canine teeth. Its tongue was dripping as it salivated in anticipation. Then it stopped and dropped even lower, wiggling its rear end as it engaged its back legs in readiness for action. It had selected its victim, which was blissfully unaware of the predator closing in, as it moved away from the group foraging for tasty plants. The jaguar saw its opportunity. It crept closer and closer, remaining hidden and silent. Then, in a flash, the cat exposed itself, charging at high speed towards its prey. The peccary turned and ran squealing after its friends. But it was doomed. The cat was fast and determined. It pounced on the little mammal, piercing the peccary's skull with its knife-like teeth, bringing instant death to its prey.

Robyn gasped and her heart pounded in her chest as she witnessed the raw power of the jaguar. The peccary was helpless in comparison. Although it was majestic, Robyn found it upsetting to watch, but she couldn't have turned away even if she'd wanted to. Her eyes were glued to the spectacle as the cat dragged its dinner into the undergrowth until it was out of sight. Robyn breathed deeply and tried to slow her heart rate. Paprika gave her a comforting peck on her shoulder. "Don't be upset, Robyn, this is how life in the jungle is meant to be. The cycle of life is wonderful when it's left as nature intended. Did you notice how quickly it was over? The peccary wouldn't have suffered much. The fright of the chase would have been worse, as it wouldn't have known anything once the jaguar pounced."

"But I can't help being sad for the little wild pig and its family. It was probably only a youngster, and its mother will be devastated," Robyn said with feeling.

"Yes, it's hard to accept. But it's the cycle of nature, and we have to focus on how amazing it is. Let's move on. You're not going to like what you see next but I have to show you, as this is part of the training process."

Robyn looked worried and downcast. "Oh no, I don't want to see upsetting things."

"Robyn, I wouldn't be putting you through this if I didn't think you could handle it. One of the reasons you were chosen is because of your sensitivity, and love of animals. And your love for this beautiful world. You are a fantastic candidate for the cause, so just be strong. You won't remember this on waking; the pain is temporary."

"Okay, I'm ready – anything I should know first?" Robyn asked.

"Only that you stick right beside me, and if I move, you move – don't hesitate or question, just do it – quickly."

Robyn eyed her friend with trepidation, but managed to say, "Okay, I'm right beside you all the way."

CHAPTER NINETEEN

They flew well above the treetops for about half an hour. They went deeper and deeper into the forest. Eventually, Paprika slowed and glided down onto a firm branch atop a tall tree. "Do you recognise that sound in the distance?" Paprika asked.

"Yes, I think so. It's a chainsaw or, rather, lots of them," Robyn replied in a worried tone.

"Afraid you are right. This area is supposed to be protected by law. But as I said earlier, the government can't keep track of all the illegal logging." Paprika took off again towards the frightening noise.

Robyn immediately followed her mentor. She didn't want a repeat of the penguin episode when she hadn't stayed close. As they neared the sound, she heard the terrified cries of the birds and other animals of the forest. Paprika and Robyn flew over a hill, and Robyn cried out. It felt as though her heart was being squeezed in a vice. She got such a shock that she forgot how to fly. She plummeted like a plane out of control.

"Robyn – fly! Robyn – come on, fly!" Paprika yelled as she turned and dive-bombed after Robyn. Paprika swooped down below Robyn, screaming at her to fly.

Robyn remained in a daze as she headed for the denuded forest floor at an alarming rate. Paprika flew below her and stretched her wings as wide as they would go, trying to catch Robyn to slow her fall. With a thump, they impacted. It seemed like their wings would tangle and they would fall together to their deaths. But the jolt of Paprika's body against hers brought Robyn back to her senses. She spread her wings, lifted her head and dropped her tail, which acted like a parachute, slowing her descent.

"Fly, Robyn!" yelled Paprika again as she curbed her own descent by flapping her wings, encouraging Robyn to do the same. Robyn flapped her wings crazily, managing to steady and save herself just a few metres from the ravaged forest floor. They swooped up and back towards the hill and found a safe resting-tree.

"Are you okay, Robyn?"

"I think so. I'm sorry, Pappi. I got such a fright when I saw all that machinery and all the animals trying to get away. I just panicked and forgot that I needed to fly. Are you okay? You hit me pretty hard."

"My wing is a bit bruised, but it'll be better within a few seconds. I just need to rest for a moment and let my body heal itself," Paprika replied calmly.

"Thank goodness you are so quick and smart. Thank you for saving me. I could sense the fear from all the animals and birds. Those poor sloths will never get away in time. And all the birds with nests in the trees, they can't save their babies. And what about the monkeys and the insects? Even those nasty looking tarantulas? And what about the frogs and the wild pigs and the jaguars? Will any of them get away?" Robyn sobbed as she thought about the poor creatures whose lives were in jeopardy because of humans.

"Some of them may manage to flee deep into the forest. Of course, there is no hope for the babies and the nests. Many of the smaller and slower creatures won't make it out. Sometimes, as the animals panic, the men put out traps to catch them to sell as pets. It's disgusting. These loggers destroy the forest so fast, and it is lost forever. The animals, birds and insects that lived here can't ever return. It is likely this will be burnt and then cultivated for crops or cattle. Many species are threatened by extinction if this doesn't stop soon."

Paprika spoke faster and faster. "Not only is the wildlife threatened but so are the plants. If people continue to rape the planet like this, even humans will be in danger. Think about the lack of oxygen from the loss of all this greenery. And the knock-on effects of global warming. Then there's gold mining. That means more deforestation. And the toxins end up in the rivers, polluting the waters and killing the fish. Our magnificent planet is being poisoned and destroyed."

"Oh Paprika, I am sorry. I feel ashamed to be part of humankind sometimes. People can be so cruel and uncaring and so greedy and just... well, just plain stupid," Robyn apologised to her friend as she saw how agitated and upset Paprika was becoming.

"Robyn, you are not like this. There are so many of you who are beautiful, loving and caring people. You mustn't apologise for all those short-sighted, greedy and careless beings. Some of them don't even realise what they are doing. They have to work to look after and feed their families. And then there are others who are just plain evil. They don't care what or who they hurt to realise their selfish gains. I am sorry to expose you to this, but you can't feel it the same by watching it on TV or the Internet or by reading about it. Now you have experienced the creatures' terror, you have first-hand knowledge about the devastation of our flora and fauna. You will better understand Earth's ecosystems. You will know how important it is that every creature and plant, and especially man, plays a part in preserving its delicate balance. Otherwise, Earth will be in serious trouble."

"I'm feeling so overwhelmed and tired and sad. It was

all amazing until we flew over that hill and saw the devastation. I don't think I can even fly. Can we please go home now?" Robyn asked. Her voice quivered with emotion as she looked at her friend with sadness in her eyes.

"I understand. I feel the same. We'll go home now, and I will give you a break from the dreams for a while."

Robyn felt the now-familiar spinning as Paprika gazed intently back at her. And then thankfully everything went quiet and dark.

CHAPTER TWENTY

Robyn reached over to the alarm on her cellphone to switch off that awful racket. Five o'clock. What was she thinking last night when she set her alarm to go off so early? She sat up and Paprika rushed over to her, licking her hand and making soft whimpering sounds. Robyn felt terrible. Her throat was dry and her arms heavy and stiff, as though she'd done strenuous new exercises. She felt sad and depressed and had a slight headache. "I hope I'm not getting the flu," she said to Paprika as she stroked her dog's soft ears.

Paprika jumped up onto the bed and snuggled into Robyn as though she understood that Robyn wasn't feeling so good. Robyn stroked Paprika's silky coat. "You aren't supposed to be on the bed, Pappi. Come on, off you get, and you must go out to the toilet."

Robyn dragged herself out of bed and opened her bedroom door to let Paprika out. Paprika rushed downstairs. As Robyn climbed back into bed, she heard the doggie-door knock back and forth as Paprika went outside. Robyn decided that she could have at least another hour's sleep as there was no way was she going for a run this morning, feeling like she did. She reset her alarm for 6:30 and pulled her duvet back over her. Next minute Paprika was all over her, licking and nudging. "No Paprika. On your bed. Go back to sleep." Paprika lay down on Robyn's bed, pretending not to hear. Robyn pushed her with her feet and growled, "Off the bed – now." This time, Paprika responded and leapt off Robyn's bed and onto her own.

It seemed like only moments had passed when Robyn's alarm buzzed again. She switched it off and sat up. Her door was open and Paprika wasn't in the room. Robyn remembered that she'd left the door open earlier. "Pappi," she called, and whistled. Paprika came bursting through the door and leapt onto the bed.

"You are getting naughty jumping on my bed all the time," Robyn said with a laugh. But she loved having her on the bed. It was her mum who wasn't so keen. "Let's go for a quick walk." At the word 'walk', Paprika was off the bed, down the stairs and waiting at the front door in a flash. Robyn got up and realised she was feeling fine, so guessed she had just needed a little extra sleep. Maybe she wasn't getting sick after all.

They had a twenty-minute walk around the block then, after feeding Paprika, Robyn got ready for school.

Robyn felt much better this morning with Hayley back at her side, and the day went okay until the end of the second class.

As they headed for the door as the class finished, Gina deliberately bumped Robyn, knocking books out of Robyn's arms. "Hey ghost-face, watch where you're going," Gina said and turned away, laughing with her friends as Robyn's face flushed and she bent down to pick up her books.

Hayley knelt next to her and whispered, "Don't let her get to you."

"Hey Robyn, let me get those for you," Ryan shouted, loud enough for Gina and her friends to hear.

Robyn stood up, relieved that Ryan was around.

"Thanks Ryan," she said.

Gina spun back towards them with a scowl on her face as she realised Ryan was helping Robyn. Robyn could see that Gina had not expected that as part of her plan, and she felt a ray of hope.

Hayley grabbed Robyn's elbow to guide her through the doorway towards Gina. Hayley deliberately stopped between Gina and Ryan. She gave Gina a sickly-sweet smile and twisted back to Ryan. "Ryan, you're the man." Hayley nudged Robyn as Gina huffed and walked away.

"Round one to us," said Hayley. "That was easy. This is going to be fun."

Ryan handed Robyn's books to her. "Don't worry about Gina, Robyn. I'll look out for you."

Robyn was gobsmacked. She didn't see that coming. How embarrassing. Ryan must know about the drama. She felt her cheeks flush again. This was getting ridiculous. Every time she saw Ryan, she seemed to blush. It was pathetic. What was wrong with her? She managed to say, "Thanks Ryan," as she took her books from him and rushed off, trying to hide her confusion.

Hayley ran after her. "What's got into you? You're acting so weird. Oh my goodness – you're blushing. You've got the hots for Ryan."

Robyn snapped back, "Don't be stupid. I haven't."

"Ooh, now you're getting snappy with me. It must be true. Have you got the hots for Ryan?"

"I'm sorry, I didn't mean to snap at you. I don't know what's wrong with me. I'm so emotional. I can't get through a day without blushing or crying, or both. I'm a mess. And no, I don't have the hots for Ryan. I hardly know him, but I do like him. He seems like a decent person."

"Hey, I'm just teasing you. You're going through some tough stuff with this drama you had with Gina. I'm just trying to lighten the mood for you. Anyway, it was great that Ryan came to the rescue. Did you see Gina's face? She was so peed off. It was awesome."

In their next class, Sarah sat with Robyn and Hayley. Things seemed to be returning to normal. A couple of the other girls who had ignored Robyn last week, said "Hi Robyn, how are you doing?" and smiled at her sheepishly.

"What did you say to them, Hayley?" Robyn asked.

"I just told them to catch a wake-up. That they know you'd never say vicious, vindictive stuff about anyone. And I told them that they'd hurt you by avoiding you."

"Oh Hayley, you shouldn't have done that. I feel so humiliated," Robyn said.

"It's them that should feel humiliated for believing dumb rumours," Hayley replied. "They are all so scared of Gina and her group. What's to be scared of? What power does she hold? Is she going to kill everyone for not agreeing with her? Hardly. She's just a bully. And because she's good looking, she gets away with it. Everyone seems to idolise her. Dumb, dumb, dumb."

"You make it sound easy to stand up to her. I'm glad you're on my side. What did the others do when you said that to them?" Robyn asked.

"They agreed. They are all scared of Gina. They don't even know why. It's actually quite funny. They doubted that you would say things like that, and they shouldn't have believed Gina. They agree with me that Gina is jealous of you and they said they are sorry to have hurt you."

"Wow, Hayley, you are amazing. Thank you for being such a good friend to me. But I have no idea why Gina would be jealous of me."

"Robyn, you really don't know do you?" asked Hayley.

"Know what?"

Hayley laughed and ran her fingers through a lock of Robyn's thick, blonde hair. "You are so gorgeous and you have absolutely no idea that everyone thinks that. You are very special, and it seems that you are the only person in the world that doesn't realise it. And that's probably one of the things that makes you so adorable. You are so naive."

Robyn looked at her friend in shock and then felt her face redden, yet again. To hide her confusion, she nudged Hayley and said, "You talk such rubbish sometimes, but it's so good to have you around. I missed you so much."

Robyn got through the day with relative ease, with her best friend once again at her side. All her other friends were back with them, and it felt good. At lunchtime she noticed that Gina's group appeared smaller than it had last week. A few girls had broken away from Gina's group and were sitting in smaller groups of two or three girls. Robyn smiled with relief. Things were getting back to normal.

The Calling

CHAPTER TWENTY ONE

Robyn was still outside kicking the ball to Paprika at nine o'clock on this lovely evening. As Robyn turned eastwards the full moon was rising, squashed and orange, just above the horizon. It was enormous and cast a soft magical light over the trees and shrubs. The sky was cloudless and the stars had dimmed in deference to the moon's glory. Robyn took a deep breath and stood quietly, in awe of her universe, as she wondered about what could be out there among the zillions of stars.

Paprika seemed to sense her wonder and moved closer, leaning gently against Robyn. The night was heady with the scent of her dad's flowering creeper wafting on the breeze. The potent smell, and the glow from the moon, lulled Robyn into a trance-like state, and yet with heightened senses. Time seemed to stand still. Although her sights were on the rising moon, the trees in the garden appeared to be in perfect focus. Paprika's fur was soft and silky against her bare legs. The haunting call of a morepork beat a spellbinding rhythm. What a magical evening.

A flash of bright light broke the spell as it shot down

like lightning, straight towards Robyn. Her body reeled for just an instant. Then she was being pulled up at an insane rate through the night sky. The trees and shrubs flashed by her as she rose crazily upwards. Even through the weirdness, it struck her as being odd that she didn't feel any changes to her body – no pressure like she would on some of the rides at the amusement park – that g-force effect. It was as though she was still standing in the exact position she had been in when the flash hit her, even though she was ascending rapidly. She could still feel Paprika's fur rubbing against her leg. She looked down and got a shock as she couldn't see her body. Nor Paprika. Only the vista of a fantastic moonlit world, right where her feet should be. It was as though her body had disappeared into thin air. She reached up with her right hand to touch her face – thank goodness she could feel it. But her other senses seemed to have disappeared. She realised she couldn't hear anything. She was enveloped in total silence such as she had never known. There was no longer any scent hovering in her nostrils. And where was that sense of movement?

It was bizarre. She should have been terrified. But she wasn't. She was, in fact, relaxed and, for some strange reason, felt safe. Just as that thought occurred to her, everything went black. Pitch black. Total and complete darkness. Now she started to panic. Almost immediately the sound-vacuum lifted. She heard Paprika's voice whisper in her ear, "Relax Robyn".

That familiar voice instantly calmed her. A split-second later a soft golden glow enveloped Robyn. As her eyesight returned, and she could once again see her feet and her legs, she breathed a big sigh of relief. She could even smell the lingering perfume of the creeper once more. She was surprised when she felt a warm and gentle human touch on her left arm. The golden light expanded and she turned her head.

Standing beside her was a young woman. Her hair hung

in shiny russet tendrils, shot through with shades of light-auburn and gold. The curls near her face were pale gold. She was tall, slim and athletic looking. She was wearing tight-fitting dark-brown leggings and a beautiful golden tunic, which was adorned with exquisite sparkling gems. As Robyn looked into the eyes of this lovely woman, she grinned. She immediately recognised those amber eyes, rimmed by long dark-brown lashes. Her gorgeous dog was now an even more gorgeous human being. Her world got crazier by the minute. Paprika's human skin was faultless and glowed like satin, with a golden hue. Her soft, rosy lips parted to show beautiful, even, white teeth as she smiled at Robyn. Robyn's heart flipped in wonder and she gasped, "Oh, Paprika, you look like an angel."

"In a way I am your angel, Robyn," Paprika replied, as she put her arms around Robyn and hugged her gently.

Robyn's whole body tingled with good vibrations. She was astounded at the feeling of love that surrounded her. It was a sensation like she had never known. She was aware of a calm, accepting, forgiving, trusting and pure, unconditional love emanating from Paprika. It was a love that gives all and expects nothing in return. Not only did Paprika look like an angel, but she made Robyn feel as though she had been touched by an angel.

As Robyn accepted this magical sensation, she looked around. The golden light expanded further to reveal her surroundings. They stood in what appeared to be a glass tube in the centre of a small room.

"How are you feeling, Robyn?"

"I feel wonderful. Better than I have ever felt. This must be heaven," Robyn replied with a huge grin on her face, as her heart fluttered with joy.

Paprika nodded and the glass tube vanished. They stood on a slightly raised golden platform. The walls of the small room faded until they were almost invisible. Robyn's surprised face reflected back at her. There was a goddess standing beside her. And beyond their reflections was space. Literally. There was darkness and then stars. Zillions of stars. She was awestruck.

The room rotated and dipped slowly. Robyn gripped Paprika as the floor beneath them tipped. Fascinated, she realised she wasn't going to fall over. It was as though she was glued to the floor. Beyond the glass walls was a spectacular vision. Earth, in all its wondrous glory, was spread before her, like in pictures taken by space shuttles and satellites. Their craft was so high that it must be almost in orbit. Lights twinkled along the east coast of Australia and the long islands of New Zealand. Robyn was dumbfounded. It was unbelievable. It was inconceivable. It was brain-numbing. It was mind-boggling. It was stunning. She was spellbound.

Paprika touched a gem on the wrist of her tunic, and the platform they were standing on expanded. It formed a semi-circular padded seat with a high back, in front of which was a glass console. Above the console floated a prism. It looked like a diamond encrusted with amazing gems, resembling those on Paprika's clothes.

"Well Robyn, the process has begun in earnest now. You have passed all the tests that you have been put through and we are now going onto the next phase. Sit down and relax." Paprika pushed an orange gem on the prism. A panel rose from the console with two small glasses filled with a translucent golden liquid. Paprika passed a glass to Robyn as they sat down. "Have a drink of nectar from the heavens."

Robyn took a sip and thought she must indeed be in heaven. It was the smoothest, sweetest, tastiest and most thirst-quenching drink she had ever had. She felt an exquisite sensation as each droplet ran smoothly down her throat. Immediately she felt alert and focused. "That's the most delicious thing I've ever tasted. I feel like I am ready to handle anything now."

"That's good, because this is going to be pretty hard to take in. I can finally tell you who I am. You're not going to believe it, but hang in there as it'll get stranger before it makes sense," Paprika said, watching Robyn closely. "Call me your angel, if you like. I don't live on Earth, but I am human. I'm here to guide and mentor you."

CHAPTER TWENTY TWO

Robyn gaped at Paprika. She opened her mouth to speak, but nothing came out. It was ludicrous. She was going insane. These night-time excursions were now right over the top. This seemed different from the other dreams though. It felt more real... in a weird way. Maybe it felt real because she was human still? And what did Paprika mean that she didn't live on Earth, but she was human? An angel? Robyn was totally confused and her thoughts were going around in circles.

Paprika laughed. "You look surprised. I thought you said you were ready to handle anything?"

Robyn still couldn't speak.

"I shouldn't tease you, but you look so shocked. You're extremely confused now, aren't you?" Robyn nodded. Paprika continued: "You do remember the other dreams you've had, don't you? You recall being with me in various places around the world as different creatures?" Again Robyn nodded, still speechless. "And you know that you didn't remember any of it on waking?"

"Yes," Robyn stammered.

"Well, so it continues. My name is Rika. It's no coincidence that you called me Paprika. But you can shorten my name to Rika now instead of Pappi – I never really liked 'Pappi'. Anyway, I digress. As I said, I am human, on the next phase of my journey. I am from Opaitu, which is an incredible solar system in a galaxy very far away from your Milky Way. I appear to you as a dog because you relate so well to dogs. And, of course, dogs are known to give unconditional love. So, it makes sense that, as a dog, I would win your trust." Rika smiled, reaching out to hold Robyn's hand. "And you are a wonderful dog-owner and friend to me. You are gentle and loving. You show discipline the way a dog needs it, so I trust you to be the alpha of the pack. You physically exercise me and play games that work my brain. It's a wonderful life being a dog with you as my friend and master, Robyn."

As Rika let go of Robyn's hand, Robyn smiled self-consciously. "This is so weird talking to you like this. But when you are a dog, I talk to you as though you are human, so I suppose it's not that weird," Robyn giggled. "You make a fantastic friend and you are such a smart dog and I have such fun with you. I feel lonely when you aren't with me. You have become such an important part of my life. You help me feel safe and I know that you do love me unconditionally. I almost feel as though you are my soulmate – that you understand me and love me regardless of all my faults." Robyn felt tears stinging her eyes as emotion welled up in her.

"Dogs often have that effect on their human masters. That is why it was decided that help would come to Earth, at this time, with an initial connection through dogs. Earth has been monitored for many thousands of years by higher beings. They have been watching over Earthlings, waiting for them to rise to their true destiny, but they aren't progressing in the way they should, and mankind and Earth are in imminent jeopardy. So, the Universe has determined that Earthlings should receive some assistance to ascend to a higher plane. However, as humans have been endowed with free-will, the Universe may not directly interfere, so you and other young people from around Earth have been chosen to help this ascension. Youngsters with qualities aligned with this evolution have been carefully selected. You are one of these special people."

"But there is nothing special about me. I worry about so many things, and I am never sure of myself. I don't see how I could possibly help," Robyn said with a lump in her throat.

"Oh Robyn, you are perfect for this mission. You are considerate and compassionate. You always look for the best in everyone and you are a wonderful and loyal friend. You are kind and gentle with animals. You care about the well-being of people, animals and the planet. You are still young so you have much to learn, but you are destined to rise into your higher self in this lifetime. And you will soon be able to help others to move to a better place too."

"Paprika... Rika," Robyn corrected herself, "I can't believe that I have been chosen. I'm not a good enough person." She sobbed and swallowed hard. "I probably won't be brave enough to do what is needed, or smart enough to understand. Maybe I just cannot do this." Tears squeezed from the corners of Robyn's eyes as her heart raced with anxiety.

"Relax Robyn," Rika said and touched Robyn gently on the arm.

A wave of calm washed over Robyn at Rika's touch. Robyn wiped her eyes with the back of her hand and took a few deep breaths as she felt her heart rate normalise.

"The world needs people like you to build a bridge between life on Earth and eternal life thereafter. It's a huge thing to try to grasp, but you will gradually comprehend and not question yourself so much. As before, you won't consciously remember what you have experienced, but you will absolutely know, deep down in the core of your being, that a better life exists."

Rika stopped talking for a few seconds to give Robyn a

chance to digest what she was saying. "Don't over-think things now Robyn, it will all become clearer as we progress."

"What just happened and where are we now?" Robyn asked.

"Remember the flash that hit us when we were standing on the deck?" Rika asked, and continued speaking when Robyn nodded her head. "That flash brought us up here into this craft, and returned us."

"What? Returned us – what do you mean?" Robyn asked in confusion.

"Well, we will actually be back standing on the deck at exactly the same time we left. In Earth terms, we won't have moved."

"I can't believe all this – I'm going nuts."

"Just go with the flow and enjoy. Like in the dreams," Rika said gently. "We are currently in a vehicle called a prisima. As you can probably tell, it's small. But it's super-fast and utterly undetectable to humans or their technology. We are going to link up with a crystalcraft soon. I won't explain more, as I don't want to spoil the joy of what you will see and experience by giving you my point of view in advance. Finish that nectar and we'll get moving."

Robyn's mind was spinning. How could she be at home and here at the same time? It was all too hard to comprehend, so she decided just to enjoy the ride. She drank the last few drops of the nectar and put the empty glass back on the console next to Rika's. Her body thrilled as the nectar flowed through it and her mind became clear and focused once more.

Rika winked and pressed a bright blue gem on the prism.

Robyn was pulled back into her seat by restraints that had wrapped themselves securely around her. The seat moulded firmly to her body as armrests extended, giving her more support. The glasses from the nectar did a disappearing act. The console morphed, curving up close to Rika so that she looked like the captain of a spaceship. Oh, that's probably what she was, Robyn realised as she took a deep breath in anticipation.

CHAPTER TWENTY THREE

Robyn felt the g-force for a fleeting moment as the little craft leapt into action. Then the force regulated back to normal even as the craft shot crazily across the night sky. She had an almost 360-degree view of everything around her. The only areas she couldn't see were where she and Rika and the console were in the way. Everything else was visible through the glass-like structure of the prisima. She could see the stars and the Moon and the amazing Earth. They were already well away from Australasia and she could see the entire continent of Africa, and it was in daylight. They were racing over Earth in mere seconds. It was incredible and spectacular. Unbelievable.

"Look at that storm over the Indian Ocean, Robyn," Rika pointed out as she pushed another gem on the control prism. The craft slowed and stopped, hovering high above Earth. Robyn wasn't aware of any changes in pressure on her body this time.

There was a spiral of white over the dark-blue ocean. Robyn could clearly see the eye of the storm as it spiralled in on itself. "Wow, that's pretty scary. I'm glad we are way above that. And look at Africa. It's as though it's been divided into three colour bands. I guess the band of tan right across the north is the Sahara Desert?" Rika nodded and Robyn continued: "Then there's all that green across the centre and towards the south. And the small triangle of tan in the south-west must be the Kalahari Desert? I'm surprised at how much arid land there is in Northern Africa. And look how big those lakes are in East Africa."

Rika nodded. "The huge one is Lake Victoria, which forms the borders of Uganda, Kenya and Tanzania. The two long lakes are Lake Tanganyika and Lake Malawi."

"This is way more fun than a geography class," Robyn grinned.

"I could carry on with the lesson, but we've got a meeting to attend." Rika touched the prism and once again they leapt across the sky.

"Woooooo, I love it," Robyn squealed in delight.

Rika laughed and nodded her head. "I know. I could get totally hooked on this."

"I'm having so much fun with you, Rika."

Rika gave Robyn a wry smile and made adjustments on the control prism. The craft smoothly changed direction. It headed north and proceeded to fly north-west over Europe. Greenland was covered in white. The inlets from the sea carved intricate patterns into the frozen mass. The prisima once again slowed as Rika manipulated the gems. They came to a stop somewhere high over the frozen land.

A flash of bright red and orange above them startled Robyn. As the flash dissipated, she saw a sparkling object. It looked something like a multi-coloured diamond. "That's the crystalcraft entering Earth's mesosphere," Rika explained. "We are in the upper ranges of the stratosphere where the air is stable. We are above where the jet aircraft fly. The crystalcraft is coming to meet us."

As it neared, Robyn could see that it was exactly like a crystal. It had multiple facets, shaped like triangles. The colours moved and changed constantly as it reflected and refracted light. "Oh my goodness – it's going to hit us," Robyn shouted in alarm.

The diamond hurtled towards them without slowing. "Nooooooooooo," Robyn yelled, flinching as the craft shot towards them, stopping only metres away.

Rika laughed at Robyn's reaction.

"Oh my goodness, I seriously thought it was going to crash into us. Phew – that was too close." As her heart rate steadied, Robyn said, "It looks like one of those polygons we were shown at school. A something-hedron?"

"Well done Robyn. It's an icosahedron which has twenty equilateral-triangle faces. It's an amazing vehicle."

Although the craft looked transparent, she couldn't see anything inside it. She heard Rika say something in a strange language as she once again pushed at the gems on her control. The craft disappeared, just like that, in an instant.

"Where did it go?" Robyn asked.

"It's still there but it's just not visible even to us anymore. It's too dangerous for the craft to be visible. It wasn't such an issue a few decades ago when only the odd person would report UFO sightings. Most of these claims were dismissed as tricks of the light or the ramblings of crazy people. The sightings have never been taken seriously so we haven't had to worry. But Earth's technology these days is more sophisticated. The rate that the craft came through the atmosphere and to a halt beside us is mega-fast. It's unlikely to be monitored even by current technology. But we have to be more careful these days, and also select remote parts of the world to arrive and leave from."

"So, in the prisima, have we been invisible all this time?"

"Yes, but not to the crystalcraft. They know exactly where we are and can see us. We need to see the crystalcraft, so I will put it on observation mode." Rika touched the console. Immediately the craft came back into view as though it hadn't disappeared.

"Wow, that's pretty awesome," Robyn cheered.

"Let me show you what our prisima looks like from the outside." Rika pressed some more gems and a hologram rose in front of them. Their craft was not a circular object at all, like Robyn had imagined. It was a little triangular prism with just three faces. As the hologram spun, the prisima also appeared to reflect beautiful colours. Just like the crystalcraft it too appeared to be transparent. Another diamond.

"Rika, how come there isn't another crew member in this craft? You boarded with me, but there was nobody else on board already. Does it fly alone?"

"Yes, it flies remotely. It gets sent from the crystalcraft with a specific destination programmed, which can be managed even when the crystalcraft is way out in space. We have incredible natural materials in our galaxy and our technology is totally mind-blowing. Earthlings have a bit of catch-up to do," Rika laughed as she shut down the hologram and focused on her control prism.

The edges and vertices of their prisima became visible around them as its faces became semi-transparent. It was as though they were sitting in a vehicle instead of floating in space. Slowly the prisima began to move towards the crystalcraft. As it did, the bigger spaceship turned slightly and then stopped. The triangular surface directly in front of them opened from the middle out, like the aperture of a camera. They glided towards the opening, and then they were inside the crystalcraft. The aperture closed behind the prisima. As they continued to float further into the crystalcraft another aperture closed behind them. The manoeuvre had been totally smooth and quiet.

Rika explained, "We are inside the main structure of the crystalcraft, in a passage along the edges where the faces meet. Look at all the other prisimas docked along the framework. That's what we are about to do." The prisima rotated slightly as one of its external edges stuck onto the internal edges of the larger craft. Rika hadn't touched any controls. It was docking automatically.

"That's very cool," Robyn remarked as she watched with interest.

"Yes, again it's thanks to the materials that we have. It's like a magnetic force. Let's check things out."

As Rika and Robyn stood up, the console and chairs disappeared. The golden platform was, once again, under their feet. A narrow opening appeared where their craft was joined to the bigger one. Their platform moved across to the opening and they were once again in a glass tube. The tube moved upwards and, after a few seconds, stopped and the glass disappeared as it had done earlier. An opening materialised before them and the platform glided through.

Robyn's sudden intake of breath was audible. Her eyes were transfixed on the centre of the room. Two, almost translucent, ethereal beings hovered above a platform facing them. They shimmered with golden light and appeared tall and thin with light-green eyes and pale, platinum hair. They had the most commanding presence Robyn had ever felt. She sensed an immediate and unusual connection to them, as though their eyes viewed her soul and they knew everything about her, better than she did herself. Robyn sensed their compassion, love and understanding. It was uncanny and totally beyond Robyn's comprehension to feel such a connection, which resembled a forceful intuition, one that was part of her very core. She perceived a deep-rooted bond with these celestial beings that was far too hard to comprehend right now. But she had a feeling she was about to find out.

CHAPTER TWENTY FOUR

"Hello again, dear Rika. And welcome to you, Robyn. It's wonderful to see you both." The deep, booming voice seemed somehow familiar. Before Robyn had time to pursue the thought, Rika stepped off the platform and moved gracefully over to the speaker. She bowed, placing both hands into his outstretched palms of glimmering gold, and said, "Hello Levi. We are humbled to be chosen for this mission. Robyn and I will work hard to serve the Universe and humankind."

Robyn nearly toppled over as she realised why the voice was familiar. Levi, the blue whale! Her whole being thrilled with excitement and anticipation at the wonders that were unfolding around her.

"We have no doubt about that, which is why you have both been chosen." This voice came from the female figure standing beside Levi.

Robyn could hardly contain her excitement as she thought, "I know her voice. That's Gwen."

The woman answered as though Robyn had spoken to her. "Greetings, Robyn. You are correct, I am Gwen. It's good to meet you again, this time in your human form. But I did enjoy watching you learn to be a penguin, and it was fun to go tobogganing with you. I don't get to do that often enough. Hello Rika, how are you doing?"

Rika smiled and bent, greeting Gwen the same way she had done with Levi. "Hello Gwen. I'm wonderful thanks, and so excited about our assignment." Rika motioned for Robyn to join her, indicating that she should perform the same ritualistic greeting. As Robyn's skin touched these beings, her heart soared with a profound feeling of peace and wonder. Goodness enveloped her.

She stepped back, gazing up at Levi and Gwen in awe. She had no idea how to address them. She had never been in such presence before, so she just smiled sweetly and said, "Hello."

They were beautiful-looking beings, similar to humans in their own shimmering, not-quite-real way. Yet they were so much more. Robyn couldn't think of a word to describe them. Then it came to her... 'purity'. Yes, they were absolutely pure. Untouched by anything that wasn't of the highest integrity or goodness. How could she sense this, she wondered? It was all very perplexing.

Levi took Robyn's right hand in his. "We are Tuerians. We are guardians of the Universe. We understand your confusion at all this. It's absolutely foreign to everything you have ever known and believed."

As Levi released Robyn's hand she smiled politely and nodded her head. She felt like a tiny little girl – ignorant and innocent. But she knew that she could place her total trust in these beings. She innately knew that they loved her unconditionally.

Gwen touched a lilac gem on Rika's tunic. "Your suite is ready. I suggest you take Robyn to rest while we wait for the others to arrive."

"Thank you, we'll see you later," Rika said.

She grasped Robyn's hand and led her through an archway that opened to the left of them. As the archway closed behind them, Rika explained, "This passageway leads to the resting and living areas. There are many interconnecting passageways like this one, so it can be bewildering. When Gwen touched the gem on my tunic, she gave me access to our accommodation. You will notice that doorways off the passages are gem-coded; it's sort of like colour-coding. The gems on the tunics control access and permissions around the craft. Come, I'll show you."

"Oh, look. That lilac gem on your tunic is pulsating. Does that mean it's our colour-code?" Robyn asked.

"Yes, some of the codes are intricate gem-patterns. The resting areas are not high security areas, so they just have a simple code like this single pulsating gem." They reached an intersection in the passageways. Rika took the left-hand passage, which pulsated with lilac lights, until she reached a door where a lilac gem flashed twice.

Rika touched the lilac gem on her tunic twice. The door opened to reveal a strange-shaped room with a transparent sloping ceiling. Two violet-coloured couches formed an L-shape that fitted perfectly into the corner. A triangular crystal table was in the open area in front of the seats. On the right side of the room was an upside-down triangular crystal prism. A sparkling counter was anchored to the prism. Beautiful crystal mugs and glasses floated above the counter.

Robyn looked up and was rewarded with an exquisite view through the clear ceiling of the room. A frozen expanse of land glowed in the early dawn light. It was surrounded by deep blue sea. The inlets reminded her of the little cracks on the first cake she tried to ice with her mum. To the south there were a few dark patches where the land had not totally frozen over. And so much water. From up here she could appreciate how much water covered Earth.

"That's the southern tip of Greenland," Rika explained.

"Oh, I expected that it would be daytime here, as it's almost mid-summer in New Zealand," Robyn said.

"Exactly. Which means it's near mid-winter here, so the daylight hours are short. It's now about 9:30 in the morning here and just starting to get light."

"Oh, right. It's all very disorienting."

Rika nodded. "Of course it is. This will be our apartment while we are on the crystalcraft." She took Robyn through to the bedroom area on their right. "There are two identical rooms; this is yours, and mine is across the hallway." On entering the room they turned to their right, to find a bathroom. The toilet and small hand basin were made out of the same sort of crystal material. Even the taps were crystal. Everything sparkled as it reflected the light. "Thank goodness the toilet isn't transparent," said Robyn with a giggle.

Rika laughed. "I'd never thought about that, but you are right, that would be pretty gross." There was a beam of blue light shining on the floor opposite the hand basin. "That's the shower. You just have to walk into the beam of light, say 'on' and the water will flow. You can command changes with your voice. Use simple words like 'hotter', 'cooler', 'more pressure', 'less pressure' and 'side jets'. Everything you need is there. You won't need a towel, 'dry' will do it. There are various commands for drying your hair when still in the shower, depending if you want to dry just with light, with light and air, or just with air. There are body lotions and perfumes if you want them as well.

"Thank you, it's all fantastic," Robyn exclaimed.

"Here's your bedroom," said Rika as she led Robyn into another room.

Against the far wall there was the most unusual bed Robyn had ever seen. It was a translucent cloud with a soft lilac sheen, floating about half a metre above the floor. Beside the bed, a small upturned crystal triangular prism acted as a bedside table. Recessed into the wall was a panel of gems or, as Robyn now recognised, controls.

On the wall adjoining Rika's bedroom was a picture of Earth as taken from space. And that was it. That was the room – nothing very spectacular, apart from the bed.

Rika smiled. "There's information about the crystalcraft on the control panel. Try out the bed."

It was at the right height to sit on, but it looked to Robyn as though it would collapse as she sat. "Go on," Rika encouraged.

Robyn gently eased herself onto the edge of the bed, making sure her legs were in a tight squat so she wouldn't fall. As her bum touched the cloud, it moulded itself to her shape and, as she took off her shoes and lay back, the bed followed her movements, supporting her all the way. She rolled onto her side and the bed cushioned up against her back. A pillow formed for her head, supporting her neck precisely.

"This is amazing, Rika. I want one of these at home." She gazed up at the ceiling which showed a view of Greenland. "Rika, we're upside down. Earth is above us. How is that possible?"

"The whole spacecraft has gravitational floors. So, no matter where you go, you will actually be the right way up. Even though you may be upside down or sticking out horizontally in relation to Earth."

"Wow, wow, wow! This is truly unbelievable."

"Reach over to the control panel and push the blue button, Robyn."

Robyn did as Rika instructed and the view of Greenland disappeared. The room went dark except for a soft blue glow which enveloped the bed. Robyn felt a soft satiny drape fall over her body as quiet soothing music filled the room. Her body relaxed and she immediately floated away into a deep sleep on her cloud in the sky.

CHAPTER TWENTY FIVE

Robyn woke to a gentle nudge on her hand. She rolled over and opened her eyes to greet her dog. Instead there was beautiful Rika with her hand resting lightly on Robyn's.

"Time to get ready," Rika said.

As Robyn sat up, suddenly aware of where she was, she felt the bed rise up behind her, supporting her back. "How long was I asleep?" Robyn asked.

"Just over an hour. How are you feeling?"

"Like I have slept for hours and hours. This bed is amazing and I feel wonderful."

Rika nodded as she pushed gems on the control panel. The blue light that Robyn remembered just before she fell asleep was replaced by a soft white light. The music changed from soothing to more upbeat tones. A door in the wall adjoining the bathroom slid open to reveal a wardrobe. "Have a shower and then you will find clothes in the wardrobe. Not much choice as you will see. There's red, red, or red, in the way of tunics, and a few pairs of identical slate-grey pants to choose from. Oh, and let's not forget the shoes – you will find those very comfortable. There is plenty of choice of gorgeous underwear though and it's all the perfect size for you. You should tie your hair up in a braid. You will find all the lotions and hair accessories you need in the bathroom. Come through to the living area once you are ready and we'll get something to eat. Enjoy your shower."

Robyn thanked Rika as she left the room and the door slid closed behind her. Swinging her legs over the side of the bed, she stepped onto the floor. The bed rearranged itself, fluffing out the indents from her body and the moulded edges that had supported her. The satin cover draped itself neatly over the bed, falling in soft folds to the floor. "That was the easiest bed-making session I've ever had," Robyn murmured. She looked up at the ceiling. The craft must have moved around since she had fallen asleep as she could now see the moon and stars. The moon's craters looked very pronounced. It seemed if she reached her arm up, she would be able to touch the stars. There were millions and millions of them. But she couldn't see any constellations that she recognised. Oh, of course, she was now in the northern hemisphere. The sky would look different to what she could see from home.

As she walked barefoot through to the bathroom, the floor felt odd. She hadn't noticed the floor at all before she slept, but then she'd been wearing shoes. She looked down. The floor looked like it was made of marble, but it didn't feel cold and hard. It felt almost like a soft carpet. Perplexed, she knelt down to touch it with her hands and take a closer look. It was a strange material. The colours changed as she moved her head. In fact, she couldn't even describe a colour. It melded into the décor of the room with a marbled effect. Robyn guessed that somehow it picked up the colour from whatever light shone in the room at the time.

Robyn walked into the bathroom, took off her clothes, threw them onto the floor, and stepped into the beam of blue light, saying, "On." The softest water she'd ever felt rained down on her head from the stars above. Well it seemed like it was from the stars, as that's all she could see when she looked up. The fine droplets danced over her skin like feathers. They created the most amazing sensation she'd ever felt from water. Her hair was immediately wet through even though the water felt too soft to soak her in such a short time. Remembering Rika's instructions, she said, "More pressure." Gradually the feathery droplets became like the touch of fingers drumming on her flesh. The intensity was perfect for a few seconds. Then it became too intense. She quickly said, "Stop." The water switched off. Robyn laughed as she realised that she probably should have used a different command to change the setting rather than stop it altogether. She got it started again, and the water came back on at the fiercer setting as she stepped into the shower. This time she got it right, saying, "Less pressure." She let it return to the original setting. This could take some getting used to. She should have checked out the info gem on her bedroom console.

Robyn held her hand under the light for the shampoo until she had a few squirts in her hand. It smelled like strawberries with a hint of jasmine and maybe some vanilla. It formed a rich lather, and then rinsed off in a flash. She finished with a pump of conditioner which had the same beautiful delicate fragrance and felt like a silk-coating on her hair. Once she'd rinsed that out, she said, "Off," and then, "Dry." Gentle waves of warm air rolled over her body. Oops, what was the command for drying her hair? She didn't remember if Rika had been specific, except something about light. "Hair lights," she commanded as she looked into the mirrored surface of the far wall. Light beams moved from the crown of her head down to the tips of her hair once, and then disappeared. She looked in the mirror, turning her head. Her hair shone with golden highlights. Something inside her snapped and she found herself dancing around the bathroom laughing hysterically. This was all too much – she was losing the plot.

Next thing Rika was knocking on the door, asking if she was all right. Robyn found a bathrobe hanging on the door. She yanked it on and between laughs called out, "Come in, Rika."

Rika burst into the bathroom in alarm. "Are you okay?" She breathed a sigh of relief as she realised that Robyn was hysterical with laughter. She wasn't crying.

"Look at my hair," Robyn giggled, finally starting to get some control over her outburst.

"Oh my goodness, what did you do?"

"Well, I didn't check out the info gem before getting into the shower and I didn't know the commands. I remembered you saying that there were different ways to dry my hair. With air or light or both, so I said, 'Hair lights'. I guess it sounded like 'highlights' in my accent," Robyn said as she burst into another fit of giggles.

"That's funny," said Rika, joining in with the laughter. "And it looks great. Which is just as well as there's no time to change it. Quickly get dressed and meet me in the lounge."

Robyn dressed in her new clothes. The material was soft and gentle on her skin, and was light and airy. The shoes were the most comfortable things she'd ever put on her feet. Her new look was impressive. She didn't normally wear red, but the tone seemed to complement her skin and new hair colour, and she looked radiant. There was a band of gems along her lower left sleeve enmeshed in the fine weave of the fabric. They looked like the gems on Rika's tunic, but these weren't shimmering. Maybe the room was too dark? Robyn's skin was glowing after her shower and her hair, though still damp, was shining. As she plaited it she noted how pretty the golden highlights were as they shimmered and shone.

She hurried through to the living area with a spring in her step.

"You look good, Robyn," Rika complimented.

"Thanks. I feel fantastic after that sleep and shower."

With a thrill of excitement, Robyn wondered what the day was about to bring.

CHAPTER TWENTY SIX

Rika turned left out of their suite. A flashing yellow gem on her tunic matched one along the passageway. It signalled that they were to follow a corridor to their right. Several metres further on, yellow lights flashed over an archway on the left. The archway opened to reveal a large auditorium.

The top level where they were standing was the shortest side of the room. This appeared to be a sort of reception area, with a few couches and tables dotted around. The room widened out on either side, then angled back in towards a large flat stage at the bottom of the room. The stage was slightly broader than the level they were on. The ceiling was transparent, as it had been in their suite, with a stunning view of the stars and inky sky. They appeared to be alone in the large room. Beautiful music played and the room glowed with soft golden lights.

Rika followed flashing lights on the floor. These led them on a sort of escalator down to the eleventh row of seats. There were eleven sets of seats in this row. Each set or pod consisted of two large seats with a control prism on the outside edge of each seat. There were gaps between each set of seats. Yellow lights flashed on the two centre seats. Rika led Robyn over to those and motioned to her to sit in the right-hand seat. As she did so, the seat moulded to her body. She wriggled and the chair adjusted to her movements until she settled. A chair had never felt so comfortable. Cool air circulated around her making her feel alert and focused, but not cold.

"Touch this button on your control," Rika said, showing Robyn.

Robyn turned to the control on her right and did as instructed. Her seat rose higher and the legs elevated until she was lying facing the sky. She pressed again and returned to her sitting position.

"And this one," Rika showed Robyn.

The button projected a hologram in front of Robyn.

"What a cool auditorium," Robyn whispered. Other people were now entering the room and moving to their seats. Robyn observed the proceedings with interest. "There are lots of young people, all with beautiful beings like you leading them."

"This is the first convention of the apprentices and their mentors. That's why the seats have been set out as they have. Each apprentice and mentor is a little apart from the next pair."

The seats on either side of them filled up. As Robyn turned to her right, she gasped, "Rika that looks like my friend Ryan, from school."

"It is. They have chosen youngsters that attend the same school or live nearby, so that they have support."

Robyn turned back towards Ryan, who wasn't looking her way. He appeared to be wriggling in his seat and testing it out. "Ryan," Robyn called quietly, hoping he would hear her.

His head swung around in surprise and his eyes opened wide. Then he burst out laughing. "I shouldn't be surprised to see you here, Robyn. When Max told me there was someone else from our school here, I should have figured it would be you. He wouldn't tell me who though, would you, Max?"

"I wanted to surprise you. Hi Robyn, nice to meet you properly, in my human form."

"Hi Max. Nice to meet you too. You make an awesome dog though, and Paprika likes you," Robyn giggled.

"Well, Rika and I go back a long way, so we should be able to get on as dogs. Hey Rika, it's cool that we can finally all meet like this and start working together."

At that moment the lights dimmed, and the volume and tempo of the music increased. The windows above darkened, shutting out the view of the stars. Revolving crystals on either side of the stage lit up colour by colour. Magical light swirled around the entire auditorium. As the lights hit the prisms next to their seats, they reflected back towards the stage. The entire room became a magical light show for a few seconds. Then the crystals stopped spinning. A beam of golden light shone onto the centre of the stage, revealing two beautiful ethereal figures who Robyn now recognised.

Levi and Gwen floated above a raised golden dais at centre stage. Without a word being said, Robyn suddenly felt serenity touch every part of her. These heavenly beings emitted waves of compassion, love and purity. It was an exquisite sensation. Robyn knew in an instant that she shouldn't question herself. She realised that she loved herself exactly the way she was, but not in a selfish or egotistical way. She understood that she was one of the Universe's perfect creations. It was humbling and moving and comforting, all at once.

Robyn looked around the room. She got the impression that everyone in the room was having this revelation. She also felt connected to every person in the room. It was strange and incredible.

Levi's rich deep voice floated around her, touching her ears and her soul. "Welcome Earthlings and mentors. Thanks to each of you for bringing your special gifts to our cause. You have been carefully selected. This is a mission that has not been attempted before, as the Universe may not change or interfere with the free-will of humans. However, life on planet Earth has become so damaged and corrupted, that mankind and all living creatures, and even the planet itself, are in jeopardy. They are in danger of complete and irrevocable destruction. But there is hope, so the Universe has decided to find a way to assist Earth and all within and upon it."

Levi paused and looked around. Everyone was riveted to his words and there wasn't a fidget in the room. He continued: "There will be no interference with people's free will. You are the chosen ones. You have all displayed an inherent goodness and love of your planet, its creatures and other humans. Tests have been performed over the last few months to ensure that you are suitable. Some didn't pass these initial tests, so are not here now. Some of you may yet not pass further tests during the next stage. That doesn't mean that you have failed. It will only mean that you aren't ready right now to take on this enormous responsibility. At any time, you may also opt out of continuing with this mission."

Gwen took over. "Those of you who don't progress through this stage will return safely to your homes. You will have absolutely no recollection of any of this. However, you will still subconsciously know that there is a better place after Earth. You may continue to serve yourselves and others through this knowledge. However, we feel sure that most of you will pass our next stage of trials and move on to further your knowledge of life after Earth."

Levi added, "This stage will take place around your planet Earth, which will be viewed and experienced from this spacecraft. For those selected to continue in stages to follow, life will be quite different, as we will go to a galaxy so far from here that Earthlings have no idea of its existence."

The room erupted with clapping and cheering. Once it

quietened, Levi continued: "We are ready to begin. If you have any questions as we go, please push the green star on your console. As you do that, think your questions as though you were saying them. We will hear these and your questions will be answered, if possible, during the course of this session. We will have breaks every couple of hours to enable you to stretch your legs and go to the restrooms. We will have a quick break now. Food will be served during the next break. Water and other liquid refreshments are available from the consoles beside your seats. You may help yourselves to these at any time. Thank you for your attention. Please return to your seats in ten minutes."

Robyn watched Levi and Gwen in fascination as they literally faded away. The room was once again bathed in soft golden light. Everyone got out of their seats and moved to the reception area via the escalators. They seemed stunned and there wasn't much conversation.

Robyn dashed off to the bathroom. On her return she found Max and Rika leaning against the back wall, deep in conversation. Robyn stopped a few metres away to take a good look at Max. He was quite a bit taller than Rika with light golden-brown hair, cropped fairly short. His eyes were dark golden-brown, framed by heavy black eyebrows and lashes. He had a straight nose and a neatly-trimmed dark beard and moustache. His smile was beautiful, showing even, white teeth. His body looked strong and muscular and he exuded confidence and energy. No wonder he made such a lovely german shepherd dog. Robyn turned to look around the room. All the mentors were stunningly beautiful, with flawless skin and shining hair. None of them seemed to carry excess weight. They all looked super-fit, like athletes. In fact, they all looked perfect to Robyn.

"Checking out all these gorgeous people, are you?" Ryan said as he approached Robyn with a grin on his face.

"Yes, they are all dazzling. They are alike in many ways, and yet each one is quite different. And they all look so serene and comfortable with themselves. Confident but humble. And although they are serene, I can feel their energy. It's as though I can actually see their inner beauty. And they all seem to be young. Well older than us, but like in their early or mid-twenties, don't you reckon?"

"They sure look young. But I have an inkling that they are really old," Ryan replied as Rika and Max signalled to them to return to their seats.

"I can't wait to see what they're going to show us," he added as he made to move back to his pod. "It's sure going to be an interesting day."

CHAPTER TWENTY SEVEN

Robyn watched the people as they sat down. It was evident that the trainees were from all around the world. There was a mix of nationalities, cultural backgrounds and races. Each was accompanied by a beautiful mentor. There was a buzz of excitement in the room. Once everyone was seated, Levi and Gwen once again appeared on the stage. This time they were sitting, as though suspended, on a cloud-like couch.

Levi began: "I hope you are all feeling refreshed and ready for your new adventure. Before we begin, I know there is a question in your minds. How is the gap in time, between you leaving home and your return, going to be explained to your family and friends? Well, there won't be a time lapse at all. We are able to transcend space and time, so you will be returned to your homes at the precise moment that you left. It will be as though you never left."

Hands went up all over the room. Levi laughed. "I know you are all going to ask how that is possible. Well, that is not for mortals to know. Even your mentors don't understand it. As mentioned before, you will be able to transmit your questions, by thought, using the green star on your consoles or your display screens. You may do this at any time. Some of the answers will not be available, but some will, so please ask anyway."

"Your consoles have been specifically designed to look familiar to you according to current Earth technology, so you will be able to follow with ease. Please press the emerald 'Display' gem on your console."

All over the room, transparent hologram-type screens appeared in front of each seat. Robyn saw they had small pictures or icons, much like her cellphone did.

"Please follow instructions. If you try to move on ahead or jump around selecting various icons, you will find that nothing happens. This ensures that we all move together through the sessions. I see we already have had a similar question posed by many of you.

"We have been asked, 'How can everyone understand German?' And, 'Does everyone here speak Japanese?' And, 'The English people won't be able to understand you speaking in Portuguese.' And, 'We aren't all Chinese – do all the other races here know Chinese?' Typically, none of the English-speaking people have questioned it. They all expect everyone to speak English," Levi said with a chuckle. "The answer to these questions is that we are speaking a universal language to you. You will all understand us as though we've spoken in your own native tongue. All your mentors converse in the same way. At this stage, students will only understand others who can speak the same language. Your mentors will translate for you."

Gwen took over. "Firstly we will show you a little more about the crystalcraft. You will have had a glimpse of it before docking so you know what it looks like from the outside. It looks rather like a ball consisting of triangular faces. Let's take a look on your displays."

Robyn looked at her screen. A picture of a crystalcraft was revolving in front of her. The triangular facets picked up beautiful colours from the light projected onto them.

"Every triangular face is a window to the outside of the craft. You will have noticed that the ceilings in your rooms are windows. We can divide the craft into three sections, like this," Levi explained.

As Robyn watched, the craft on her screen separated into three sections. The two outer divisions looked like open umbrellas, with their apexes pointing in opposite directions.

"The middle band is off-limits to you, as that is the heart of the spacecraft," Levi continued. "The outer sections, the ones that look like open umbrellas, are the living and training areas. There is a connecting elevator tube running through the mid-section to join these. You will notice that the umbrella-type faces are each made up of five triangles."

The image changed from the spacecraft into an umbrella. This revolved and tilted to show exactly what Levi was talking about.

"The 'umbrella wires' leading to the apex are the connecting structures and passageways on the craft. These join the faces, and at each apex is a control room, so we have twelve control rooms around the ship."

The image highlighted the wires of the umbrella. Then the umbrella changed back into the section of the spaceship. It revolved so that the apex was facing towards the screen. Through the transparent ship, two platinum-haired heads were visible on the screen. The heads tilted back to show the faces of Levi and Gwen, who lifted their arms and waved.

The image then tipped so that the apex pointed up. The triangular facet facing Robyn began to open like a lens, exactly as it had done when they entered the craft. A prisima moved through the opening and docked against one of the structures. Two figures emerged from the craft. They were standing on a platform but hanging almost upside down.

"The ship has two entrance points for the prisimas to enter. These are located on opposite sides of the spaceship. All the structures, passageways and internal floors on the craft have gravitational plates. These have the same force as that on Earth so, while in the spaceship, you will feel no different. Although you may be upside-down in relation to Earth, you will still feel as though you are upright. Gravity pulls down from underneath you. These plates also compensate for sudden bursts of speed. Even when the ship turns or moves suddenly, you won't feel any sudden pressure or changes in your balance."

Many trainees whispered to their mentors and nodded in comprehension. Robyn turned to Rika and smiled, "Okay, I think I understand it now."

"Either that, or I'm going crazy," Robyn muttered to herself. And the latter seemed entirely possible.

CHAPTER TWENTY EIGHT

Gwen took over. "We travel at tremendous speeds, as you will already have realised. There is no need for alarm. The ship is equipped to come into close contact with other objects without crashing. They will not touch unless programmed to do so. We may get very close to aircraft at times but we won't crash, even though we are not visible and cannot be detected by radar or any other earthly systems. Even as we travel through space, Earth is unable to track us or have any idea of our existence."

There was some whispering and fidgeting from the students.

Levi continued: "In your present state, you should all remember dreams that you have recently had with your mentors. You will have had a few experiences as various animals. Is that correct?"

There were nods around the auditorium. Robyn could make out some of the words: 'yes', 'si', 'oui', 'sim', 'ya' and many more versions of 'yes'.

Levi continued in a grave voice. "Those dreams will help you understand how it feels to be an animal on Earth. How it is in their natural environment. What it is like to be the hunter and the hunted. And how it should be without human involvement. Some of you will have even experienced the terror of being hunted by people. There is much beauty in your world, but there is far too much horror created by man. By this stage in human evolution over many eons, people should have learned more about love."

Levi took a deep breath. "Love not just between two individuals, but love for the air that they breathe. Love for the ground they walk on. Love for the rising and setting sun. Love for the bountiful oceans. Love for clouds that bring rain and life to the planet. Love and wonder for every living thing. This love should take precedence over all other emotions. And of course, humans should have learned deep respect for everything. Respect is a form of love, which projects love outwardly. But many Earthlings are so caught up in greed and lust, envy, pride, anger and apathy. They don't even love themselves. They abuse their minds and bodies. Abuse with addiction and decadence, idleness, anger, fear, self-loathing. And so it goes on. People must firstly learn to treat themselves with love and respect. Then they can regard other living beings and this beautiful world with love and respect."

His voice deepened and seemed to resound deep within Robyn. "You are mankind's hope for their future and the future of planet Earth. We understand that this is a huge responsibility for such young people. If anyone in the room feels this is too much for them, they may decline our proposal at any time during these training sessions. There is no shame in recognising that you are not ready for this, and there will be no consequences. You will go home with your mentor, who will return to his or her animal form, and you shall continue your life as normal. You will have no recollection of any of this. If you wish to leave, you may stand up now and tell us your reasons. Or if you feel uncomfortable to do that, you can send us a thought message." Levi smiled and looked around the room. "Remember there is no disgrace in your decision to leave now. It is courageous to admit that you are not ready. We applaud you, whatever you choose, and thank you."

A petite girl with glowing ebony skin, stood up about four rows in front of and to the left of Robyn. She bowed her head and said in a small voice and unusual accent, "I don't think I am the right person to do this. I am scared of all sorts of things. I was terrified in the dream when I was a rabbit and was chased by a fox. I thought I would die from a heart attack." Her voice faltered and she sobbed quietly. Her mentor put a hand on hers and immediately she calmed down.

Gwen replied, "Amanika, you are exceptional to stand in front of all your peers and tell us that. It shows courage and strength of character. It is natural to be scared and that emotion, when the fox was chasing you, is what saved you. Otherwise you wouldn't have run fast enough and taken refuge in your burrow. Being scared or unsure is natural. Bravery is displayed by overcoming that fear. You have just shown that courage by standing up in this room and voicing your concerns. I'm sure there are many of you in this room who feel like Amanika does. Would anyone else like to voice similar fears to Amanika's by standing up?"

Robyn jumped out of her seat with her hand raised, without giving it another thought. She had very similar concerns. And it appeared that she wasn't alone. Many boys and girls all over the room were now standing. They all looked around self-consciously.

Levi and Gwen both had huge smiles on their faces. "Thank you all for being so brave and honest. You are all going to be wonderful for this cause. We commend you. Be proud of yourselves and remember that we are here to help you. Unconditional love is one of the many things that you will experience on this journey. But if any of you are still in doubt about whether you wish to continue, we will respect your wishes. The lights will now dim for a few minutes to allow you to leave, should you wish. Thank you and may you be blessed with love and goodness

141

throughout your lives," Levi said, and he and Gwen sat down as the lights dimmed.

Robyn could hear movement in several places around the room. She couldn't make out how many people left the room. There must have been a few, judging by the soft footfalls on the stairs. When the lights came back on there were some empty seats, including the one directly in front of her. Robyn couldn't recall who had been sitting there. She looked over to her right to check that Ryan was still there. He gave her a big grin and a thumbs-up. She smiled back at him with relief. It felt so much better that she knew one of the candidates. Robyn was also pleased to see that Amanika had remained in her seat. It gave her courage to know that they had similar concerns but were both prepared to continue this journey... for the moment, anyway.

Robyn felt her stomach knot in anxious anticipation of what might follow. She wondered if she would really be strong enough to see it through.

CHAPTER TWENTY NINE

"We will now visit various places around the world," Levi explained. "As I mentioned earlier, this time you will be in this spacecraft and not in the body of an animal. We will start with some of the true wonders, both natural and man-made. Everything will be recorded for you to re-watch, and re-experience later if you wish to. We will see a lot in a short space of time, so there will be much to take in. Please have a glass of nectar before we commence. This will heighten your senses and concentration."

Robyn pressed the button on her control that she recognised as the nectar icon. As she took a sip of nectar, she thought how she could get hooked on this stuff. As she sipped it, restraints appeared from the seat and wrapped around her as they had done in the prisima.

Rika said, "Just to make you feel safe – there's actually no chance of you falling out of your chair."

Robyn grinned and started to giggle. She realised she had that feeling in her stomach of excitement and nerves all at once. Rika reached over and laid her hand on Robyn's. Robyn glanced to her right to see that Max had done the same with Ryan. Ryan's grin looked as though it was going to split his face. There was no doubt that he was super-excited.

The ceiling of the auditorium, which had remained dark since the light show started, now once again became transparent. The stars shone and glimmered in the darkness of space. "Doesn't look as though we've moved since we came in here," Robyn commented.

As she said that, she felt the slightest pull on her tummy and the craft spun and zoomed downwards. Robyn couldn't feel the spin on her body, but the view changed. The stars were replaced by a view of the icy Earth, coming up to meet them at an insane rate. It was like nothing she could ever have imagined. She thought they'd risen fast from the deck at home into the prisima. And even faster across the sky towards Greenland. But this was almost instantaneous. One second they were looking at the distant stars, and the next at a close-up view of moonlit ice and dark sea. Then everything came to an abrupt halt as they hung suspended a few metres above the frozen land. There had been no sound of an engine. The whole manoeuvre was in absolute silence. Even the people in the room had been silent. Now they exhaled as one.

The day had faded, so Robyn guessed they must have been hovering over Greenland for a few hours. The craft spun, revealing the night sky through the ceiling once again. The scene took Robyn's breath away. She had never seen anything as beautiful. Swirls of iridescent greens and yellows waved across the sky. These were interspersed with dark violet and deep royal-blue. Shafts of magenta struck though the darker colours. Pale yellow mists swirled around. The Northern Lights danced as though orchestrated. They lifted and fell and appeared and disappeared like mist from a genie's lantern. As melodic music matched the dancing lights, Robyn realised that the show was, in fact, orchestrated with the precision of a Royal Ballet performance. The colours changed and blended; all the while a zillion stars twinkled in the distance. A myriad of shades and tones of green swirled around. Bright teal morphed to deep blue, to plum and then to deep purple. It was magical.

The next moment they were shooting up through the night sky. The swirling lights disappeared, to be replaced by dark space and bright stars. Robyn looked at her screen. There was a replay of the light show with a caption scrolling over it:

> *The Northern Lights. Also known as Aurora Borealis. Caused by collisions between electrically charged particles from the sun entering Earth's atmosphere. Variations in colour due to various gasses mixing with these particles. Yellow-green caused by oxygen, and blues, violets and purples by nitrogen.*

Robyn whispered to Rika, "I never knew what caused the aurora – that was so awesome."

Rika smiled. "Stay tuned. I have a feeling there is more awesomeness coming."

Robyn's screen dimmed as the crystalcraft dashed across the sky, high above the Earth's surface. Within moments they were in bright daylight. The craft slowed and turned face-down to Earth, then began to descend. Slower this time. Amid a vista of blue, Robyn could make out a few small dots of white and one long white ribbon ending in a half-moon, which looked like a crooked question mark. She didn't register what it was at first, but as the craft levelled off a few hundred metres above the ground, she was able to identify a series of waterfalls. They seemed to flow in tiers from all directions.

"Wow, there are waterfalls everywhere. So much water. And look at that beautiful rainbow," Robyn exclaimed in delight. The craft slowly descended towards the water until they were totally surrounded by falling water. Some of the falls were above them and they were level with others. They drifted towards a viewing platform where people crowded, taking photos of the falls. The craft hovered so close that Robyn felt as though she could reach out and touch the platform. The people seemed oblivious to them, even as the craft spun around and flew up above the top waterfall. It glided just above the top of the falls and then plummeted down as though the force of the water had caught them. Robyn gasped and clutched onto the arms of her chair. Rika laughed. They hurtled along the falls and dropped again towards the churning water at the bottom of the falls. They must have landed on the water because now she felt as though she was in a boat, pitching and dipping, and rocking and rolling, in the turbulence of the rapids. It was exhilarating. But also confusing.

"They've changed the motion control setting so that we can feel the motion," Rika explained as she saw Robyn's confusion.

"I love it," said Robyn.

"Not everyone does," replied Rika as the girl behind them started yelling in panic. Next came the sound of retching. "Don't worry Robyn, she won't vomit on you," she added, as Robyn jerked in response.

"Thank goodness for that, I can't stand puke," Robyn gasped.

"Unlikely that she would puke on you, as a sick bag would have deployed from her console. The chair has sensors to detect things like that. Even if someone pees themselves, the chair deploys a special mat to soak it up. Our engineers are pretty smart," Rika added as Robyn raised her eyebrows. "Her chair will stop allowing motion now it senses she doesn't like it. She won't feel ill anymore."

As the girl behind her fell quiet, Robyn realised she wasn't going to get sprayed with someone else's regurgitated meal. She relaxed and grinned as she continued to enjoy a wild ride down the rapids. "This is a seriously amazing craft. I don't want this to end."

But no sooner had the words escaped her mouth than they were shooting back up into the sky. Robyn's screen lit up again with a replay of this last experience. The text rolled:

> *Though most of the Iguazu River flows through Brazil, the majority of the falls are on the Argentinian side of the border. The Iguazu Falls are shared by national parks of these countries and are designated as UNESCO World Heritage sites.*

Levi's voice interrupted: "Thankfully, governments are trying to protect this beautiful natural site. But there are other places we will visit later that are no longer protected as they should be."

Robyn's head was reeling. This was so much to take in. And there was still more to come.

CHAPTER THIRTY

The spacecraft rocketed across the sky once again. It descended towards a landmark that Robyn instantly recognised. She had seen many photos of the spectacular Victoria Falls, which formed the border between Zambia and Zimbabwe along the raging Zambesi River. These falls were quite different to the Iguazu ones, which had consisted of lots of smaller falls. These formed one huge long curtain of water. Their craft hovered a few metres above the river, upstream of the falls. Then it seemed to lower into the water and get taken at high speed by the power of the current. Robyn looked at Rika in shock. "We're above the falls this time, not below."

Robyn heard the girl behind her cry out in terror. But the next second she was laughing hysterically. Robyn had no time to think about that. The craft reached the edge of the falls where thousands of tons of water could drag them to their deaths. Robyn couldn't scream. She couldn't blink. She couldn't breathe. She froze. Time seemed to stand still. She felt the craft tip as the ceiling of their room became a mass of churning water. Then everything went black. The spell broke and she screamed. As another hundred teenagers did. The craft was suddenly a cacophony of sound – thundering water and screaming people. Then silence.

Robyn felt the craft rising as though on a cloud of cotton wool – for just a second. The craft bobbed up to the surface of the water. And there was water. And more water. White water everywhere. They were tossed down the rapids with water thundering down on them from above. Mist sprayed high into the air as they were whisked down crazy rapids and through a huge winding gorge, then under a bridge. All the while they were twisting and turning, bucking and jerking, rocking and rolling. Finally, they cruised into calmer water. Robyn sucked in a mouthful of air, as though she'd been trapped under the water for the last few minutes. She looked around at Ryan. She laughed when she saw his expression. If he hadn't been strapped to his chair, he would have been jumping up and down in delight. He was ecstatic – it was written all over his face.

"Oh my goodness – that was intense. It gets crazier all the time. What happened to the poor girl behind us? I heard her scream and then laugh like a mad person," Robyn asked Rika.

"Because she was so terrified, she was 'soothed' with sensations of happiness. Everyone's responses are recorded into what you would call a database. These are tests to see what you will be suited to in your coming roles, and whether you will make it to the next level."

The craft shot back into the sky where it settled for another replay of the action. Robyn felt exhausted by all the excitement and emotion. Gwen's gentle voice said, "How was that? Exciting? Terrifying? Exhilarating? Tiring? You possibly experienced all those feelings. It was pretty extreme. We apologise if we frightened you, though hopefully that was only momentary. Our systems would have kicked in to make it a pleasant experience for each of you. You have seen two quite different and spectacular waterfalls, up close and personal. We will now have a break for lunch and you can mingle if you wish, or just rest and recharge. Please return to your seats in an hour. We will do some less hectic viewing after lunch."

The moment they were out of the auditorium, Ryan rushed up to Robyn and, to her surprise, picked her up and swung her around. He was laughing with such abandon. Robyn's senses were on such a high she found it contagious, and laughed crazily with him until tears ran down her face. When the laughter subsided, she felt conspicuous and thought that everyone was staring at them. She glanced around the room and realised that everyone else seemed super-excited as well and nobody was paying any attention to her. She put her hand to her cheek and realised with amazement that she wasn't even blushing.

"Wasn't that the best thing you've ever done?" asked Ryan with a huge grin on his face.

"Sure was. Though, as we neared the lip of the Victoria Falls, I thought we were going to die. I am terrified of heights. I couldn't breathe, but at the same time I was totally mesmerised. I couldn't close my eyes and miss it. It was incredible."

"Yeah, that adrenaline rush was something else," added Ryan, still smiling from ear to ear. "Maybe it's a good idea that we are going to do less exciting stuff after lunch, or we're likely to have heart attacks from over-stimulation."

Robyn laughed. "Apart from the excitement aspect, just seeing the world's beauty and majesty is fantastic. It's such an amazing planet."

Ryan finally stopped grinning as his tone of voice became serious. "Yeah, I'm blown away by the power of the water. It's such a force of nature and crazy to see it like that – really puts things into perspective."

"Robyn, Ryan! Come and have something to eat," Max called to them, as he and Rika made their way towards produce that Robyn had never seen before. The shapes of the fruits and vegetables were totally unlike anything she'd ever seen and they were more than a rainbow of colours... there were colours that she couldn't even try to put a name to. Some were bright and others delicate.

"I don't recognise a thing – don't know what to eat. What's that berry-like fruit?" asked Robyn with a frown.

"We call it wondervine. You'll see why when you try it. As you put it in your mouth, close your eyes and imagine you are about to take a bite of apple pie," Rika replied.

Robyn did as Rika suggested, and as she bit into the tiny fruit her eyes flew open in surprise. "Oh my goodness that tastes exactly like Mum's apple pie. I can even taste cinnamon and custard, which is what she normally puts with apple pie."

"Fun, isn't it? Now take another one and imagine that your dad has just passed you one of those seriously yummy ribs that he does on the barbecue. You know, the ones I salivate over."

Robyn popped another berry-like fruit in her mouth but didn't close her eyes this time. She made a few closed-mouth mumbles whilst she ate. Even though the berry was small, it took a while before she stopped chewing and swallowed. With a big smile she said, "That's unbelievable. It tasted just like those ribs with that gorgeous sticky marinade that Dad does. It even had the texture of a rib and seemed to take a while to get through. It was as though I'd taken several bites from the rib and was chewing and swallowing comfortable-sized pieces. And, as I was eating, I thought I needed salad to go with it. I got my wish – a nice green salad with baby tomatoes, cucumber, radishes, capsicum and avocado. Wow. It's amazing. I got exactly what I felt like eating and now I'm really full." Robyn rubbed her tummy in appreciation.

"Glad that filled you up so easily," said Max as he gestured for Ryan to try something.

"Yay, my turn. Bet you I will need more than a couple of measly berries to fill up this body," said Ryan as he winked at Robyn.

"Okay big boy... off you go then. What's your meal going to be?" Max asked.

Ryan took a wondervine. "A juicy T-bone steak, a corn on the cob, a baked potato with a cheese and sour-cream stuffing and a pickled beetroot."

"Haha, good that you're adding some colour," Robyn bantered.

Ryan bit into the fruit and his eyes lit up. "Mmmmmmm, mmmmm, that's so good," he managed to get out as he chewed. His eyes closed and he looked as though he was in seventh heaven. He chewed, and swallowed, then chewed again and swallowed again, without refilling his mouth. Robyn thought how weird everything in her life was these days. This was just another oddity to add to the growing list of strange experiences. Finally Ryan had finished his chew session and came up for air.

"Wow, that was incredible. I got every one of those flavours and textures, but it was as though I kept going back for more, and now I'm absolutely stuffed."

Rika and Robyn burst out laughing as Max said, "Oh yeah, big boy – great appetite! How are we going to be able to keep you fed? You ate a whole berry for lunch."

Ryan shrugged. "If that one tiny piece of fruit can give you anything you want to eat and as much as you want, how come there's so much other food here?"

Max explained: "Well, you will of course ask for flavours you know, because what you don't know, you don't know. But what about all those other foods that you don't know about yet? You'll want to try them. And anyway, you can only have two wondervine berries within a certain amount of time, after which the next one you have will taste vile and you'll wish you never had that third one. It's nature's way of ensuring you don't deplete its reserves or be gluttonous. In order to remain in the higher realms of existence there are some very strict natural laws, and greed isn't tolerated like it is on Earth. But enough of that – we should make our way back to our seats."

"But wait...there's more!" Robyn laughed. Ryan's enthusiasm was contagious and she felt herself looking forward to the next session.

CHAPTER THIRTY ONE

The two friends and their mentors took their seats back in the auditorium. Robyn was excited to see what the afternoon session would bring. The ceiling of the room was dark and she had no idea where they were in relation to Earth now. The lights dimmed but there was no sign of Levi and Gwen on the stage this time. Robyn's console lit up with a map of Africa with a highlight over the Victoria Falls. She assumed that must mean that they were still above the falls. As the room darkened, the ceiling once again became transparent, letting some natural light into the room and confirming that they were indeed high above the falls. As she watched they moved closer and closer to the falls. They were descending fast. Robyn couldn't feel any motion from their descent and there was complete silence as everyone was transfixed. Suddenly the silence was broken as the girl behind Robyn yelled out, "Noooo, not again!"

Levi's strong calm voice surrounded them. "Relax, we are just going to show you something interesting." Robyn heard the girl breathe deeply, as Robyn also felt the wave of calm envelop her as Levi spoke.

The craft slowed as it neared the water. There were six

people sitting on a rock beside a pool of water right near the edge of the falls. Robyn couldn't believe her eyes as she watched one of them jump from the rock into the pool. He was crazy. He must be suicidal. He disappeared from sight as he went under the water, and she watched the edge of the falls in terror, expecting to see his body dragged over the edge, against the rocks and then into the churning water below. But he popped up in the pool and flung his arms over a ledge of rock at the edge of the pool right above the falls. He stayed clinging to the rocky ledge while the next person jumped and then the next, until all of them were sitting in the pool.

Gwen's voice filled the room. "Devil's Pool. Jumping into the pool can only be attempted during the drier periods of the year. After heavy rains it would be suicidal, as the lip of the pool wouldn't stop the force of the raging water and they would be pulled over the edge with the fast flow."

The craft lifted away from Devil's Pool and, in an instant they were racing high above the Earth's surface. Gwen's voice floated around Robyn. "We are now travelling towards the southern tip of Africa. That great big hole in the ground that we are now passing over is known as 'The Big Hole'. This massive crater is over two-hundred metres deep and about forty metres of water has accumulated in it. Diamond mining here started in 1871, with prospectors using picks and shovels. Several years later the various mines consolidated to form one big mine, and the result was this huge crater. The mining in Kimberley has since been closed but the area remains active as a tourist attraction."

After a quick look at the crater, the ground below them became a blur for a few seconds and then the craft once again slowed, coming to rest with an exquisite view in front of them. Robyn immediately recognised it from photographs she had seen. The harbour of Cape Town was in the foreground, with the circular structure of the soccer stadium behind, greenery to the right of it, and behind that – towards the mountain – were lots of buildings. It was a beautiful clear day and the top of Table Mountain was not obscured by the renowned 'tablecloth' of low clouds, so they had an amazing mountain vista. Some distance in front of it was what looked to Robyn like a brown eagle with wings extended, fringed with black.

Gwen's voice interrupted her thoughts. "The region that looks like an eagle from this view-point is in fact the 'lion'. The area nearest to us now is Signal Hill. As we move around, you'll see the centre part which is Lion's Rump and closer to Table Mountain is Lion's Head. The peak on the far side of Table Mountain is Devil's Peak."

Their craft dropped down towards the base of Table Mountain and then hovered beside the cable car as it ascended to the peak of the mountain. The crystalcraft spun slowly as it moved upwards, emulating the motion of the cable car. Gwen said, "This is what the people in the cable car will be seeing. Isn't it beautiful? We know a few of you in this room have actually been in that cable car and have all absolutely loved the experience. Some of you even had the pleasure of experiencing it at sunset. This is one of Earth's truly majestic places and, through man's engineering capabilities, many people have been able to visit this amazing place. Some people choose to hike up to the mountain top, instead of taking the easier option."

They reached the top of the cable and the cable car disappeared into the docking station as the crystalcraft continued alongside the peak. Robyn couldn't help but draw a quick breath in awe of the stunning beauty before her. There appeared to be a wonderful balance of nature as well as development. It was apparent that the buildings at the top of the mountain had been built with harmony in mind, as they seemed to blend in with their surroundings. The mountains appeared so unspoiled, but looking down one could see that Cape Town a popular place for people to live, as she saw the city spread out below.

Looking to the west, the deep blue of the Atlantic Ocean faded into the distant horizon. She'd heard from her mother and father how beautiful this place was, as they'd visited Cape Town. Now she was seeing it for herself. It was a pity that she'd never be able to tell them she'd been there. The craft dropped down alongside one of the faces of the mountain where there was a group of people suspended from a dizzying height as they abseiled over the edge.

As Robyn watched a couple jump out into nothingness, her heart leapt and she said to Rika, "I'm not sure I would be brave enough to do that."

Ryan overheard her. "I'd absolutely love to do that."

"Yeah, but you're crazy. You do all sorts of insane stuff and you have no fear of heights at all."

The craft followed the contours of the mountain and then flew eastwards towards the airport. Gwen's voice once again filled the room. "We are about to reach the informal settlement or shanty town known as Khayelitsha. Life is hard for these people and unfortunately there are too many places like this around the world."

The mood in the room changed abruptly from joy and wonder as the huge squatter camp came into view. Robyn was shocked at the immense size of the settlement, and the squalor and obvious poverty. Homes were made of bits and pieces of whatever materials could be found to give some sort of protection from the elements. Huge mounds of rubbish seemed to be everywhere and there were no trees or plants. Tears stung the back of Robyn's eyes as her heart went out to the poor people living in such terrible conditions. It struck her how very fortunate she was to live in such comfort and she felt a pang of guilt as she realised how much she took for granted.

As the craft lifted back into the sky the windows dimmed, shutting out the view. A spotlight in the auditorium lit up the face of a very dark-skinned boy, whose expression looked like a deer caught in the headlights. He had a pink scar across his left cheek. His eyes were wide and he was totally still, as though in shock. Gwen said, "Everyone, this is Songezo. Songezo and his family live in Khayelitsha. Songezo, would you please tell everyone a little about your life there?"

It took a moment before he responded. Songezo then took a deep breath to steady himself, stumbling over the English words. "My mother, good woman. Ten children. Me, number eight. My father, he drink lots. Strong spirits make in township. Come home drunk. Beat her. Sometime beat me and brothers and sisters. He go job in city. Money from job he take for drinking. We all so hungry. Sister she crying so hungry. I go walking streets to look work. Hot, hungry, weak – long way I walk. I walking nice area. Lots nice houses, big gardens. I sit, rest. Head down. Feel wet on arm. Little brown dog. He lick my arm. He lick again then he run up street. He stop, look back at me. I sit – I so tired. He come back, he lick arm again. He run up street. He stop, look back at me. I sit. He come back, lick arm, run away. I think he tell me go with him. I tired but get up. Follow little brown dog. His tail wag. I talk to little dog. He bark at me. He wag tail more faster.

"We walk to end street, we turn more road. We walk. He stop outside gate. He sit on grass by road. I sit by little brown dog. I touch him. He soft. He warm. He nice. I like little dog. He look at gate. He bark. He bark lots. Boy like me – not so dark like me, come from house. Skin not white. Not black like me. Light brown colour. He in uniform for school. He smiling and shouting, 'Dubs, you came back. Mom, Dubs came home.' His mother she come from house and mother and boy thank me to bring dog home. They say me to go inside to have water and food. Mother make me sandwiches and give fruit. I never eat so good. I smiling now. Big smile. She say I want work in garden for pay? 'Yes, yes, yes' I say. Little brown dog he save me. I much thank little brown dog.

"I work in garden for day. David mother pay me

money and give food for family. They ask I come again tomorrow. Every day. Many weeks. Lots do in garden. Me like earth and trees and plants. Many weeks now I work. Little brown dog follow me. All day, Dubs he follow me. He good dog. I so lucky, get job with good family in suburb.

"David he now friend. He teach me English and I learn better read and write. I never go much school. Have looking after my family. Other big sisters and brothers, they gone now. They not come back. No want see father. David family give me food. They good people. I work hard. I want get better life for me. For little brother and sister. No more live like that. My mother very sick now. Think she dying. When she die, I take brother, sister away. Not let father beat us no more. Now stay look after mother. When she die no more stay. Father bad man. Bad man. Me not be like father. He very bad man. Lucky me go with nice dog. He show way out of bad life."

Songezo sat down shakily after telling his emotional story, but he now had a big smile on his face.

Gwen said, "Thank you Songezo for sharing your story with us. We understand how hard it is for you to talk about it."

The other boys and girls stood and clapped.

Once the noise had died down and everyone was seated once more, Gwen continued: "Songezo, you are a very brave and decent young man with a good heart and pure intentions. You are in the right place, here with us now, and we know that you will be a solid part of this team. While you are here, you will be assisted with your desire to better your use of the English language. Each of you will have the chance to gain the knowledge of something you desire that can be taken back to use in your daily lives."

"Wow. I don't know what I would ask for. Maybe to be good at maths?" Robyn laughed. "That would give everyone a surprise. They would really believe I'd been to outer space if that happened." Then she thought about Songezo's story and felt ashamed of her flippancy.

CHAPTER THIRTY TWO

The room filled with beautiful music. It had a haunting lilt to it, but there was a soothing and calming quality about it. Robyn's heart went out to Songezo. She couldn't even begin to imagine the kind of life he had been brought into. Life was so unfair. She had been very fortunate to be born into a middle-class family where there was always good food to eat, and plenty of it. She lived in a safe and comfortable home with running water and electricity, she was getting a good education, and so much love surrounded her. It really hit her now just how lucky she was. All young people should have the opportunities that she had. And there she was worrying about stupid stuff like being teased about how pale her skin was.

The music continued for a few minutes, in which time Robyn felt her body relax. She hadn't realised how tense she'd become while Songezo was talking.

"Thandi, would you care to share your story now, please?" Gwen asked.

Thandi stood up and looked around the room. Her body and voice trembled as she tried to find a place to start. Her mentor put a hand on her arm and Thandi began to talk: "My father is a game ranger in Kenya. He is working to protect the animals, particularly the rhinos, which are being poached for their horns. I was with my dad one day when he was called out to investigate a section of the game park. It was horrible. I wished I hadn't been with him. What I saw I can't undo... ." Thandi's shoulders started shaking as her body was wracked with sobs. "I can't do this, I can't tell you." Tears streamed down her cheeks as she collapsed into her seat and put her head in her hands.

"I'm sorry to put you through that Thandi, and thank you. Dali, please take Thandi to the Golden Room. She won't want to be here for the next part of our journey." Once Thandi and Dali had left the auditorium, the craft descended and the windows became transparent again.

They were looking out across the most amazing landscape of brown and green scrubland in the foreground, with outcrops of trees dotted around. Beautiful giraffes were gracing the land as they stretched their long necks towards tasty new leaves that only they could reach. Herds of zebra grazed together – it was sometimes hard to tell where one zebra began and another ended with all those stripes.

Elephants swung along in long rows. There were many different-sized animals, from huge heavily-tusked oldies to the gorgeous babies running to keep up, little trunks swaying from side to side as though they had no control over them.

As the craft flew on, they saw many species of buck, hyenas, buffaloes, wildebeests, lions, cheetahs, vultures, eagles and all sorts of little creatures scurrying around. It was fantastic... and all this with the most magnificent backdrop of Mount Kilimanjaro with its icing-topped crater. Robyn's awe of Earth rocketed yet again. But that feeling was short-lived. The craft slowed and zoomed in on something happening right in front of them.

There was a spectacular rhino standing in a clearing. Its ears were pricked as though it had heard something.

Robyn could see three men on the fringe of a copse, with rifles aimed directly at the beautiful creature. The rhino was facing towards them, but the men were very still. The rhino, renowned for having poor eyesight, probably couldn't see them. The next minute Robyn saw the huge creature drop. Dust lifted around it as its massive body hit the ground with force. It had been shot by a pro. It was felled with a single shot to the head. The three men rushed in as the animal was in the throes of death, body twitching its last ever movements. They were laughing and jumping with joy as they brandished huge knives and cut into the rhino's face to remove the horns. Blood spurted all over them, which only seemed to drive them to greater delight. They leapt and punched the air in elation, holding the tusks up in victory.

Robyn's stomach knotted as she tried to keep her lunch down. She was appalled and horrified at the cruelty of these men. She felt ashamed of the human race. How could anyone be so cruel and sick and disgusting to do that to a living creature? She couldn't comprehend it. And all for financial gain. Robyn's body shook with grief as she felt tears streaming down her face. Even though she didn't want to look at the horror of the scene in front of her, her eyes were drawn back to it. The men were running off, laughing and leaping with their prize, leaving the carcass of the poor animal bleeding into the earth.

Then a scream ripped itself from her lips as Robyn saw a baby rhino walk over to the stricken adult and nudge it to get up. The baby walked around and around the dead rhino until it finally lay down with its head on the dead adult's leg. Robyn was shocked beyond belief. She felt as though she was part of the tragedy, almost as if she had participated in the killing by not taking action against the poachers. She felt physically ill and exhausted.

Gwen's voice eased over them as the windows darkened and the horrific vision was closed out. "We apologise to all of you for exposing you to that terrible scene, but it's important that you feel this emotion deep within your beings, so it will translate into your passion and commitment to help the plight of the animals and Earth during your waking hours."

Levi's voice took over. "We are going to break for the day now as you have all had a very emotional time. Your bodies and minds may be in shock and you'll be battling to take it all in. I suggest that you go back to your rooms and rest. You'll find plenty of music available that will help to settle any turbulent feelings within you. There are gyms and pools if you wish to do some exercise. The water in the pools has great rejuvenating minerals, so that would be a good option if you are feeling tired. Thank you all for your attention today and we wish you a relaxed evening and a good night's sleep in preparation for tomorrow."

CHAPTER THIRTY THREE

After swimming several laps, Robyn and Rika floated in the soothing water of the pool. Robyn slowly felt the tension leave her body as the minerals relieved her taut muscles. Rika told Robyn that although she'd seen poaching before, that episode left her feeling raw and wounded.

"How are we ever going to be able to stop those monsters from murdering Earth's beautiful creatures and Earth herself?" Robyn asked Rika.

"I don't know, Robyn. It's something that you all have to work on. A way needs to be found soon though, before some of these endangered species are lost forever. And the planet is in serious danger. If it doesn't get a chance to recover soon, there will be nothing left to fight over. It's incomprehensible that greed seems to overpower everything. The rich get richer, and the masses and the planet suffer as a consequence. I can only think that humankind has to stand together as a single race of decent beings against the minority of evil souls. A few bad people have too much power over the masses. Perhaps that is what needs to change – the balance needs to tip so that the majority of humans, who are decent people, should have the power. But how will you bring that about? That's what you are all destined to work on. Time is becoming critical though. Tomorrow's events will highlight that. For now Robyn, just relax and try to enjoy the healing sensations from the water. If you are still feeling bad in another ten minutes, I will take you to the Golden Room where Thandi went earlier."

Robyn couldn't get the picture of the mother and calf out of her mind. She swam more laps, doing several sprints to push her body so her mind would go blank. But it wouldn't. She kept visualising the rhino standing majestically one second and dead in the dust the next, with its tusks brutally ripped from its head. And that poor little innocent calf not understanding what was happening. It was soul-wrenching and she couldn't let it go. She pulled herself out of the pool with tears streaming down her face again. Her heart was being squeezed by a fierce grip and she started shaking. She collapsed onto the poolside deck in a heap, her body wracked with sobs.

Rika was at her side in an instant. She gently lifted Robyn from the floor and carried her in her arms as though she weighed nothing. Robyn was aware that she was being carried along a passageway. The next thing she was aware of was that she was lying on a golden cloud with soft golden lights all around her. Her body and her hair were dry and she was no longer in swimming gear – she was in a soft golden robe that caressed her skin like satin. The band around her heart had released and she was not sobbing or feeling stressed. She was warm and comfortable and totally at peace. She still felt the horror of what she had witnessed, but now she was coping with the emotion instead of letting it consume her. She was focused and knew she would take this experience into her inner being to serve her to be stronger and move forward and help to make a difference. How that would happen, she had no idea. But she trusted that her subconscious would find a way, however small and insignificant it may seem at the time.

Rika held out her hand to Robyn, who gladly took it as she sat up. "Are you feeling better, Robyn?"

"Yes, and thank you so much for helping me and bringing me here. I feel able to cope now. It's a strange sensation that I am still upset but have the emotions under control. Something I'm not so good at normally."

Rika smiled. "Glad you are okay now. I understand what that did to you. Many of the kids in the auditorium were badly affected. Three of the girls even decided that they couldn't continue the programme and have chosen to return to their lives. They won't remember anything from this experience. The boys seemed more able to cope with the violence. That's probably because they are slightly desensitised due to society's expectations. A couple of the more sensitive boys were badly affected and, in all, fourteen of you needed to use the Golden Room."

"Oh," was all Robyn managed to reply.

"You need to get a good night's rest as tomorrow will be another emotional day. We'll go back to our suite and get some dinner now and then you can listen to some music if you wish. The timing's a bit odd with us crossing over the Date Line and moving north and south. We'll end up only having about five hours to sleep, but you'll sleep wonderfully in that bed – as you know."

Robyn's tummy growled. "Guess I'm hungrier than I expected. I'll be happy to eat and get some rest. Today was seriously exhausting, with so much excitement and emotion. And of course, just trying to take it all in is pretty hectic. Lead me to the food. I can't wait to see what we'll have for dinner. It's not like there's a supermarket around the corner."

CHAPTER THIRTY FOUR

Once they returned to the suite they had quick showers and, as Robyn walked into the kitchen area, two exquisitely decorated lavender-coloured plates rose through the prism.

Robyn gasped in delight. "Wow," she said, as she bent closer to inspect all the items on the plate, not one of which she recognised. "Oh look, Rika, the plate is in the shape of the crystalcraft."

"Yes, and there's a reason for the fact that all the delicacies on the plate range within the violet and blue scale of the colour spectrum. The Universe speaks to us in many ways, and the natural food source from our world is filled with special properties depending on its colour. After your emotional and insightful day today, you require as much help as you can get to cope and move forward. Blue encourages calm, peace, truth, understanding, compassion and recovery, while the violets will help stimulate intuition, universal flow and wisdom. Added to those are many more such benefits, and the nutritional power in each of these little morsels is mind-blowing compared to what you have on Earth.

The plate was sectioned into five equal triangles, meeting in the centre where a beautiful miniature midnight-blue tree seemed to be rooted in a little mound of violet soil. Tiny golden droplets clung to the little branches like dewdrops on a tree in the early morning.

In the first triangle, two pale blue, almost transparent, shimmering balls, with little dark blue petal-like shapes on the inside, were grouped together.

In the second triangle were bright magenta twirls, all twisting and turning around themselves, like multiple figures of eight, linked to each other to create a complex latticework.

Triangle three was a mass of little sticks all criss-crossing in a pile that looked like a tiny bonfire stack. They were in various shades of blue and violet with a rough texture like bark.

In the fourth triangle was an arrangement of miniature segments that resembled tiny oranges but these were a bright cyan colour. Each little pocket appeared to be bursting with juice as they glistened and shone. As Robyn looked more closely she realised that these segments were arranged in the letter 'R'. As she pointed and laughed, Rika said, "I was waiting for you to notice that. It took you long enough."

"It's all so incredible. I can't wait to taste everything."

In the last triangle, little thumb-nail sized, velvety-smooth, dark-maroon flowers were sprinkled randomly. Each flower had five petals with an ice-blue centre and long golden stamen and stigma.

"Follow me," Rika said as she walked through to the lounge area, carrying the plates and glasses of nectar on a crystal tray.

Robyn noticed that the low coffee table, now covered in a golden cloth, had been raised to a comfortable eating height and was now closer to the couch. Rika placed each plate beside forks and spoons wrapped in large silky violet-coloured petals, and slid into the seat.

As Robyn sat next to Rika, she asked, "What's that little golden stick beside the plates?"

"It's a wand. Watch... ," Rika replied as she picked up her wand and, with one end facing downward above the centre of her plate, she gently tapped the other end. A fine mist of minute golden droplets sprayed down onto the plate.

"Oh my goodness, that's so beautiful," Robyn said as she picked up her wand and tapped it over her plate. "It looks like fairy-dust. Not that I've ever seen fairy-dust, but I imagine it would look like that."

"It's gorgeous, isn't it? It's not just for show either. Those droplets will help you to process what's happened today. This liquid is taken from the ovule of one of the precious plants that grows on Opimar, which is one of the planets in the Opaitu solar system. These droplets are treasured as they are full of magical properties, and we only use them in very special, magical circumstances. Today they have been given to us in celebration of your initiation into the magic of our world. "Congratulations, Robyn. You have progressed through to the next stage," Rika said as she raised her glass and drank a toast to Robyn. Then Rika pushed one of the little blue balls onto her spoon and popped it into her mouth. She sat still, without chewing, as her mouth turned up at the edges in delight.

Robyn followed Rika's lead, but she couldn't resist biting into the little ball. It cracked with a sharp noise and a delicious, mildly bitter, toffee-flavour swirled around her mouth for a couple of seconds. Then the flavour was gone and she became aware of the petal from the inside of the ball, sitting on her tongue. It was as though her mouth had become a hundred times more sensitive and receptive than it had ever been. She noticed a silky-smoothness to the petal and a very subtle minty flavour. The petal gradually dissolved on her tongue leaving freshness, as though her palate had been cleansed in anticipation of the next delight. She looked over at Rika with a grin and waited to see what Rika would select to eat next.

"For the optimal flavour experience, you should eat in an anti-clockwise direction around the plate, though you can do it any way you like – it's different depending on which order you eat them in, as they complement each other in different ways. Leave the other blue ball until last."

Robyn copied Rika in selecting a dark maroon flower from what Robyn had thought of as triangle number five – now number two – as they were working around the plate in the opposite direction to her automatic clockwise mindset. She used her fork to gently pick up the whole flower and pop it into her mouth. This time she managed to keep still and wait for it to do its magic. Suddenly her mouth 'lit-up' – that was the only expression she could think of – it was like a fireworks display of flavour as bitter, sour, salty and tangy sensations flew around her mouth.

Next were the cyan segments, which had the texture and acidity of citrus fruit, but they had so much depth of flavour they tasted like orange, then lemon, then lime and then grapefruit. Robyn screwed up her face as the grapefruit hit, then there was a sweet burst of mandarin to finish.

Robyn couldn't believe she was already starting to feel full. She'd only eaten a few tiny morsels of food. Next was the bonfire... these little sticks tasted like the smoothest chocolate Robyn had ever tasted. Within the chocolate were nutty flavours, then berry flavours, and she couldn't even begin to describe all the other tastes.

The magenta twirls were sticky and almost doughy. "Those are something like that dessert Mum makes, but about twenty times better. That's not saying I don't think Mum's desert is the best I'd had, before now. This is just absolutely, mind-blowingly, fantastic. Rika, that was unbelievable thank you," Robyn added as she popped the last blue ball into her mouth. "And I can't believe how full I am. Seriously that plate of food was probably less food than one apple, but so tasty and so filling."

"Welcome to my cuisine world," Rika smiled and added with a wink, "and that's just a taste of what's to come – pun intended!"

Rika took the plates and tray over to the console, where they disappeared from sight. She then selected some music which piped through the room in beautiful tones and rhythms. Robyn felt herself swaying to the music and, as the beat and tempo picked up, she could no longer sit. She was up on her feet dancing in a way she never knew she could. Her whole body seemed to ebb and flow like fluid. She saw that Rika was doing the same and it looked fantastic. She was a goddess. As she swung her head from side to side, her hair swirled around her like flames. Robyn couldn't take her eyes off Rika, but she also couldn't stop her own movement. It was as though her body had taken on a life on its own. She laughed at that thought.

Next thing Robyn was singing to the music. She never sang. She couldn't sing. She was totally tone-deaf and sounded like a foghorn when she tried to sing, so how was this happening? It was wonderful and very liberating. Maybe Rika had drugged her? No that was ridiculous she thought, as she realised that, although she seemed to be in a type of trance, her senses were also crystal-clear and she was doing this because it made her feel good. Rika was also singing. They were both just making sounds, not actually singing words. Rika's voice was much deeper than Robyn's and the two voices seemed to blend perfectly – *a match made in heaven*. Robyn again laughed at her thoughts as she suddenly realised she was now actually singing those words. And so was Rika.

Words of a song burst out of her. It was a song that Robyn had never heard, but she continued to sing all the words along with Rika and they were harmonising beautifully. Robyn's skin prickled with goosebumps at the thrill of it as they danced and moved around the room in perfect unity. The tempo of the music slowed and the words started to fade, then the song was over and another piece of calming music filled the room.

Robyn felt wonderful – better than she had ever felt in her life. She felt free to do what made her feel good in this instant with no concerns about how anyone else would perceive her. It was so liberating.

She was now swaying gently to the pulse of this new piece of music and was humming quietly in tune with it. She felt a peace within herself like never before. She felt beautiful on the inside and out, with a clear calm mind, with none of the usual arguments going on inside her head. Her whole being seemed to be in a place of tranquillity, yet she could feel immense energy all around her. It was as though she was part of that energy, but it wasn't frantic and confusing and stressful – it was magnificent, pure and perfect energy that encompassed everything.

The music faded out and Rika said, "You sing and dance beautifully Robyn."

"Must be the food and that fairy-dust that did it. You know I can't normally sing."

"Well, you did a good job tonight. I think we should get some sleep now as we've got another big day ahead. I'll call you in plenty of time to prepare yourself. Sleep well." Rika gave Robyn a big hug.

Robyn floated off to her room and onto her bed of clouds. She closed her eyes and immediately drifted into a deep, restful sleep.

CHAPTER THIRTY FIVE

Back in the auditorium and ready for the new day, Robyn was refreshed and energised after her beautiful evening and a few hours deep sleep. But she was also concerned. "Rika, I just don't understand how people can be so cruel. It blows my mind that one being would intentionally wish to cause harm to another – whether it's man or animal. Although the animal kingdom can be violent, it's generally about basic survival. Surely if we lived in more harmony, caring about every living thing on this planet, we'd find that there is enough for everyone?"

Rika nodded her head. "You are spot on, Robyn. This is what I mean about you having an innate goodness. If only man knew what he could accomplish and what is waiting out there once he achieves his soul's purpose and perfection, he would realise how ridiculous his current existence is."

Robyn looked at Rika questioningly. "What's out there, Rika?"

"Oops! I forget that you don't know what's out there. Hopefully it won't be long before you can see it for yourself. It really is a utopia, and I only know about a tiny fraction of it. Just believe and know in your heart that by continuing to live your life with love and respect for yourself, others, and the entire planet, you will experience it soon. Actually, you may get there before your Earth life is over, being on this mission. But you will have to wait and see."

Robyn smiled. "I shouldn't have asked that question. I know you aren't allowed to tell me. I can't help wondering though. All those stars... ."

"I know, and what you can see from here is miniscule. Anyway, come on, we need to return to the auditorium for the next session. Are you okay?"

"Yes, I'm ready to continue... I think," Robyn replied as she marched towards the door.

As they entered the auditorium, Robyn saw the young girl with the beautiful ebony skin, who had stood up to say she didn't think she could be part of the mission. "Rika, I'd like to go and speak to Amanika."

"Good idea. I haven't met her mentor yet, so it'll give me a chance to introduce myself to her."

Robyn walked towards the petite girl and smiled as their eyes made contact. Amanika's face was angelic as her white-toothed grin lit up her face.

"Hi, Amanika. I'm Robyn. I wanted to tell you how much confidence you gave me by standing up and telling everyone that you didn't think you could do this. I felt the same. Totally out of my depth and wondering why they would select me. Thank you for sharing your doubt – you were so brave to do that."

"Hi Robyn. I was so scared. I don't even know what made me stand up. I would normally just sink into my seat and pretend I wasn't there. I'm glad I'm not the only one who was feeling like that, though. And thanks for letting me know and coming to say hi."

Rika caught Robyn's attention as she raised her arm and pointed towards the seats. "I'm pleased that we've met. Maybe we can get together soon – looks like they are about to begin."

"Sure, that would be great. See you later," Amanika grinned, and both girls turned to follow their mentors to their seats.

The view from the outer reaches of the atmosphere was exquisite. Robyn would never get enough of this. The Earth was an incredible place. The various hues of the ocean-blues and the different colours of the land were amazing. The way the clouds swirled around the planet in patches, some whispers of white and, in other areas, cauldrons brewing up big storms. With a slight pull on her stomach, Robyn watched as they shot down through a light dusting of clouds, and then back into the bright sunlight.

Stunning Pacific islands came into view. As they got closer a collective gasp was heard from the room. As the craft flew low over the ocean and beaches they saw a shocking sight.

Levi spoke in a concerned voice: "This should be crystal-clear turquoise water, home to a multitude of marine life. But it is now a huge garbage patch. This floating mass of plastic, nets and other debris that you can see, is only a small part of the problem. Much of the plastic has been broken down to microscopic bits that threaten the existence of the ecological system and of life as we know it on Earth. These once-golden beaches are now the burial ground of by-products of man's so-called civilisation."

The cameras zoomed in close to a patch of debris. "What you can see now is the skeleton of a seagull, whose insides are full of man's rubbish – plastic bottle caps, fish hooks, bits of twine from fishing nets, and goodness knows what else."

The craft suddenly spun away from the island and moved out to deeper water. It dived and plummeted down into the ocean's depths. Several boys and girls screamed. The tension in the room was extreme. Robyn was in shock. Her mind was still trying to process the horrors she had just witnessed, and now they were going to drown.

CHAPTER THIRTY SIX

"Don't panic," Gwen said in a soothing voice which appeared to calm everyone instantly. "The crystalcraft can handle this. Just breath normally. We won't be underwater long. We just want to show you some more of your planet."

Robyn sighed in wonder as a pod of about twenty dolphins swam past. Their bodies were sleek and shining. They moved with such grace and beauty. What amazing creatures they were. The craft followed them for a while and then the water started churning and she could sense panic among the dolphins. One of them had become entangled in a fishing net. It was thrashing around trying to free itself, but each movement wrapped it tighter in the net. Another dolphin nudged its nose up towards the net trying to find a way to help, but this one appeared to be wise to the dangers and backed off. High-pitched squeals and crying could be heard from all around them as the other dolphins frantically swam around their tangled friend. One by one they peeled away to the surface for air and came back. The dolphin caught by the net began to slow its struggles as it tired.

Robyn sobbed loudly as tears flooded down her face.

She was horrified. She turned to Rika and cried out, "Please help it." Rika's expression mirrored Robyn's. She too was shocked by the scene.

Rika shook her head sadly. "We aren't allowed to interfere."

Robyn wanted to run away. She tried to unbuckle her seatbelt, but it appeared to be jammed. She didn't want to watch. She closed her eyes and screamed with frustration and shame. When she opened her eyes again, the dolphin was alone. It had drowned and it was now swaying gently in the ocean's current, tied by man's marine noose.

Rika touched Robyn's hand. Rika's face was tear-stained and her shoulders shook slightly as she took in a deep breath. "Oh, Robyn, I'm sorry. I didn't know that was going to happen. I'm as shocked and upset as you are."

Rika's touch triggered Robyn to action. She pressed the button on her console to send thoughts to Levi and Gwen. "Why wouldn't you save it? I know you have the power to have saved it. And you were right there. I thought you were different – I thought you were here to help and that you were good and pure and that you cared. But you obviously don't, or you would have saved that poor animal."

As the crystalcraft torpedoed up through the ocean and back into the outer reaches of Earth's atmosphere, Levi's voice washed over the room. "We are deeply sorry you had to witness that. We know how it affected each of you and we understand your accusations. Many of you have questioned why we didn't save the dolphin. Yes, we have the power. But we may not interfere. If we had done so, we would have committed a Universal crime. That would have had incomprehensible and irreversible repercussions. But this is exactly why we are here with all of you, now, at this time. We can no longer ignore the destruction and chaos that people are causing on Earth."

Levi paused to allow the room to settle. "Now is a

good time to expand on what we have already told you. We mentioned before that mankind's ascension is not happening as it should. The technical skills are progressing way too fast in comparison to the soul-path. And technology is not being used advantageously. That's perhaps rather broad – of course amazing things have been done with technology, but there is too much power for destruction, which the people in power do not seem to care about. It needs to change.

"Let's take a scenario – we will call the offender A and the victim B. A nuclear bomb is launched by A, who has different beliefs to most of the population of B. Why would they do that? What is the benefit? Do they want the land? If so, they have just obliterated it – so that wasn't a great idea. Do they want to wipe out people with other beliefs? If so, why? Because they are fearful? Why? Because they want to take over? Why? Now here's a curved ball... . A lies geographically south east of B. The nuke causes a reaction in the Earth's atmosphere. The wind direction changes and A is now down-wind of B in the path of the nuclear fallout. A becomes ill or dies from the fallout (A being, people, plants, animals - everything). But no worries, the leaders of A are rich and they were able to get out of the way of all this disaster. They travelled to a remote place that would be safe. So, who suffers? Everyone except those who decided to launch the bomb."

Levi continued: "I admit that may seem a bit extreme or ridiculous. You will probably be wondering what my scenario has to do with what we've just seen? What I'm trying to portray is the devastating power of the so-called 'advancement' of mankind. Add that to the power of individuals – whether they be countries' leaders, heads of corporations, or radicals – and we have a recipe for imminent worldwide disaster.

"What is the answer? The answer is mankind, with the emphasis on 'kind'. Kind in this context meaning decent. And it starts with you young people. You have the power.

You are Earth's future. And you need to get involved. There is no time to waste, or to sit on the fence.

"You know about the Universal decree regarding humans' free will. We have to use that in a positive way to encourage people to ascend to the next level of existence before it's too late. That's where you all come in. You will need to find ways to get mass support of ideas of how to better look after Earth and yourselves, and how to fast-track to the next level. Think of it like a game. You have all reached a plateau – let's say the end of Stage 3 in the game, but you just can't find the way through to the next level. You begin to wonder if the developer perhaps didn't even program another level. As a team, you brainstorm ways to get through. By working together, you realise that it's the power of numbers that gets you through. It's about working together as one with a common goal, and believing that you can do it. Does that make sense?"

As heads nodded enthusiastically around the room, Levi continued: "In the case of ascension, it's about working towards a goal that you cannot yet see. You have to believe in yourselves, and the power and decency of the human race, to actually enable you to get there. As you begin to get others thinking and acting with love and respect towards each other and the planet, so momentum will build until you will all be so strong and good and decent that the entire Earth will have the opportunity to move forward. In doing that you will save yourselves and your planet. Those who are not ready to ascend will at least have the basis from which to do so, and may manage it in their next lives or ones thereafter, with a healthy planet to nurture them and all that co-exist on Earth. It doesn't matter what religion, race, gender, age or colour you are. This opportunity is here for all mankind – it is what you are expected to do. It's part of the game, the journey, the experience, the learning – whatever you want to call it; life on Earth is just a drop in your vast oceans compared to what's waiting out there for each and every one of you. I can promise you, it's worth loving for."

CHAPTER THIRTY SEVEN

A new scene opened up across the front of the room as they flew over a massive desert. Even at their considerable elevation, the gold and red sands stretched completely across their field of vision, the dunes creating dark shadows. As they descended, Robyn could see ridges in the sand caused by the wind. There was a myriad of patterns and colours – it was beautiful. And now there were unusual rocky outcrops and, in the distance, she could see an oasis ringed by palm trees.

Their vision zoomed in towards the sand where a lizard appeared to be dancing, lifting one foot after the other to try to stop them burning in the hot sand. It looked kind of funny. Then it took off at high speed across the sand and paused. The sand in front of it exploded as a snake shot out towards the lizard. There was a gasp from the youngsters in the auditorium. The snake had been entirely hidden under the sand, with just its eyes uncovered, watching out for prey. The lizard didn't stand a chance as the snake sunk its teeth into it. A short scuffle ensued with the snake victorious. It swallowed the lizard whole and then dug itself back into the sand, tail first, to digest its meal.

At lightning speed the craft moved east and then came to a halt over a disturbing scene. Robyn assumed they were somewhere in the Middle East war-zone. Below the craft, the street was in shreds. Pieces of concrete cluttered the street. Holes gaped in buildings. There was shattered glass all over the road. Tendrils of smoke curled from smouldering cars. Fighting was still in progress. Six or seven young men with rifles crouched behind the burning cars, trying to find protection. Another group of armed men hid behind less-damaged buildings further down the road. Flashes of gunfire burst between the two groups every few seconds. A huge roar filled Robyn's ears. The men crouching behind the cars were thrown high above the street as the explosion hit them. Legs and arms tumbled down, body parts cast aside like trash. Lives and loved ones extinguished in an instant. The screaming started. Screams of pain in the streets below and cries of shock in the spacecraft. The horror belonged to them all.

Robyn's body shook in reaction as she cried out in anguish. Tears streamed down her face and she clamped her hands over her mouth. She swallowed hard to stop herself from throwing up. But she couldn't tear her eyes away from the grisly scene. The world below was moving in slow motion. As the spacecraft swept around behind the blast area, Robyn's heart plummeted. Behind a large piece of broken concrete, a small child and its mother came into view. The mother was wailing and pulling at the child's right arm. She couldn't budge the child. The little boy's leg was pinned down by rubble. His face was criss-crossed with cuts and blood. His left arm ended at the elbow. The mother yelled at her child. Frantic, she pulled and pulled at the child's right arm. She didn't seem to realise that her child wasn't going anywhere. Even to Robyn's innocent eyes, it was clear the little boy was dead. A rivulet of blood oozed from behind his head. His dark brown eyes seared her soul as they sightlessly looked into hers. It was as though Robyn was standing right over the boy. She was so close to them. The connection between her, the boy, and the mother, was palpable.

A sharp pain struck Robyn's chest as the mother finally realised that her son was gone and threw herself over his little body. Robyn shook with heaving sobs of distress. Finally, the mother dragged herself off the little boy's body. It was the saddest thing Robyn had ever witnessed, as the mother sat and gently lifted the little boy's bleeding head onto her lap. Whimpering, she rocked back and forth with the life-blood of her child draining into her skirt. Robyn instinctively reached out her hand as if to touch the woman, to let her know that she felt her pain and that there were people who cared. Robyn felt such a strong link with the woman that she wasn't surprised when the mother raised her face as though looking right at her. Her eyes were dark pools of despair. Robyn reached out as if placing her hand against the woman's cheek. She could sense the dampness of her tears mixed with fine grit from the blast. The woman took a deep, shuddering breath and closed her eyes.

Robyn whispered, "You are not alone. I am so sorry for your loss. There are people in the world who care. Be strong." Tears streamed down Robyn's face but, somehow, she managed to keep her voice steady. Robyn closed her eyes and she felt the same reeling sensation she had experienced in her dreams.

When Robyn opened her eyes, she was lying on her cloud-bed, with Rika standing beside her looking concerned.

Robyn's eyes glanced up to the ceiling. They now looked down on Earth from a great distance. It appeared so beautiful and peaceful. How deceitful. A wave of anger washed over her. All that beauty turned into so much pain. For what? She didn't comprehend. What were they fighting over? Did they even know why they were fighting? How could a human being take the life of another? Especially the life of an innocent child? How could someone cause such pain to a loving mother?

Anger boiled in Robyn as she felt her gut twist in reaction. She felt as if she had been involved in the murder of the young boy because she had watched without doing anything to stop it. She had never, ever felt such rage and self-loathing. Rika touched her hand. Love subdued her anger. Robyn didn't know how Rika did that. Ripples of compassion, tenderness and grace surrounded her.

She sat up with a jolt. With that touch from her angel, Robyn understood. "Rika, I can see why I had to witness that. It has confirmed something I have always known deep down. Maybe I can put it into words now. Hate, greed and anger are man's enemies. The enemy is not the person with a different religion or belief system, or one with a different-coloured skin, or one who speaks a different language, or whatever prejudices appear to create hate towards others. The enemies are the actual emotions of hate, greed and fear themselves. Those emotions twist the soul, causing bitterness and loathing, self-hate and sorrow. Then man takes these emotions out on others, causing pain and fear to be transmitted to others. It's like a virus feeding on innocent people, mutating and multiplying as it feeds. And it spreads."

Rika nodded. "Yes, I think you are right, and you are helping me to understand. Hate, greed and fear are like an epidemic. If humanity showed compassion and love for others, there would be no need for those other destructive emotions. Love would cause the rampant disease to be slowed and finally halted, reducing suffering on Earth."

Robyn's face clouded over as she murmured, "I don't think I can be on this mission, Rika."

Rika's eyes opened wide in surprise. "But you just said that you understand."

"Exactly. And I don't have the strength to deal with all the hate and anger. I can't even figure out my own emotions and understand why I get hurt and upset so easily. Look at me, I couldn't cope with what we have witnessed. How can I possibly help others?"

Rika took in a shuddering breath. "That's just how I felt when I was asked to be part of this mission. Mostly I didn't want to come back to Earth. But I also didn't see how I could possibly help. However, I decided to keep an open mind and, luckily, I had Max around. He makes everything seem so easy and non-threatening. He doesn't let things get to him. It's almost like a game to him and just another experience to enjoy. I'm not saying that he doesn't take this mission seriously, but it's the way he tackles everything. Even if it's not all enjoyable he looks at the big picture – that it's all part of our learning experience. If I hadn't bumped into him on the day we were asked to help, I don't think I would be here now."

Robyn bowed her head. Her body trembled as tears dripped onto her hands which were now clasped tightly in her lap. Even Rika's gentle touch on her hand couldn't ease the anguish that consumed Robyn. "Rika, I can't do this. Please take me home."

"Of course, Robyn. Please wait here. I will communicate your decision to Levi and Gwen. I won't be gone long."

Robyn's thoughts churned as she watched Rika leave the room. Her head was in a spin and her heart ached. She wanted her old uncomplicated life back.

CHAPTER THIRTY EIGHT

Her emotions in turmoil, Robyn lay on her bed staring blankly at her ceiling of stars. Then grief took over again. Tears streaked her cheeks and rolled onto her pillow. She thumped her fist against her thigh in frustration at her helplessness. She had lost control. She was pathetic. It was such an honour to be invited to help with this incredible cause, but she couldn't find any reason why they had chosen her. She was useless and couldn't figure herself out, so why would they need her help? She mulled it over and over in her mind, but she knew that it had to be a huge mistake. She had to go home. This was not only ridiculous, but it was embarrassing too.

"Robyn, can you come out?" Rika knocked gently on the door.

"Hang on, Rika. I'll be with you in a minute." Robyn dragged herself to the bathroom mirror. The face that stared back at her looked even more pasty than usual. Her eyes were red and puffy. She looked ill. She felt ill. She threw cold water on her face and blew her nose. She opened her bedroom door. Rika was standing right outside the door. "Oh, Rika, I didn't know you were waiting here. I thought you'd be in the lounge."

"I wanted you to know that you have visitors."

Robyn gasped, "I can't see anyone like this."

Rika wrapped her arms around Robyn and gave her a gentle squeeze. Then she stood back and cupped Robyn's chin in her hands. Robyn felt a warm sensation at the top of her head, as though a ray of sunshine was bearing down on her. It flowed down the back of her neck, across her shoulders, down her arms and into her fingertips. Then another wave of warmth spread across her chest, into her abdomen and down her legs. She glanced down at her toes as she felt them tingle with warmth, to see a shimmering golden light hovering over them. The light disappeared as Rika took her hands off Robyn's face. Robyn took a deep breath as Rika led her back to the bathroom mirror.

"What about now? Can you face your guests now?" Rika asked.

Robyn's skin was glowing with a golden tinge. The pasty complexion was gone and her eyes were bright and focused. She grinned as she realised, not only did she look better, she felt it too. "Thank you, Rika. I think I can face them. Who is here?"

"Come and see," Rika said as she led the way to the lounge.

Robyn expected to see Levi and Gwen, so was slightly taken aback and flustered when she saw who her visitors were.

"Hi Robyn," said Max with a big grin. "I hear you don't like our company."

Robyn wrung her hands together and shifted her weight back and forth. "No, it's not that."

"I'm teasing you. Rika thought you'd like to spend time with some awesome people right now. So here we are." He nudged Ryan, who stood up and walked over to Robyn, and gave her a quick hug.

The tension was broken as Robyn giggled because, for

the first time ever, Ryan actually looked uncomfortable. It was generally her in that position.

"Rika told us you want to leave. Please don't go. We need you."

"I can't do this, Ryan. They made a mistake when they picked me. I'm of no use to them," Robyn responded.

"Rubbish. You are exactly right for this mission. You have so much compassion."

"I'm weak and can't control my emotions. How could I possibly help anyone else when I'm such a mess? Rika has to keep calming me down."

"Robyn, from what I have seen and what Rika has told me, it appears as though you don't give yourself nearly enough credit," Max interjected.

"I totally lost the plot when I saw that rhino slaughtered, and then the little boy. I can't handle such cruelty." Robyn explained.

Rika added, "Which is *exactly* why we need you. You are so passionate about decency and kindness. If there were more people like you on Earth, Robyn, it would be a much nicer place."

"I'm sorry, I really can't help. I know I'm not strong enough. Please understand that I've made up my mind." But even as she said this, Robyn had the feeling that she hadn't had the last word.

CHAPTER THIRTY NINE

Max glanced at Rika, who nodded. "Robyn, I have been given permission by Levi to share some more information to encourage you to remain with us. He is convinced that you will be one of the keys to the success of this mission. And, Levi is never wrong. I know as I've been around him for hundreds of years. He is all-knowing and he is goodness and love personified. I will explain a little about him and our world. Come over here and sit next to me."

Robyn smiled hesitantly. "Ok, I'll listen as I'd love to hear more about you and your world. But it won't change my mind." She sat next to Max, who then jumped up and knelt in front of her, taking both her hands in his. Rika did the same with Ryan.

Robyn looked at Ryan. She was confused, but Ryan's eyes were alight with anticipation. She took a deep breath and relaxed.

Max began: "I'll start briefly with some of my story. I finally made it to Opaitu – as our particular utopia is known – when I died as a child during the Great Famine. You won't believe it, but I was actually somewhat of an angel, looking after my mother who was pregnant during the famine. I found a job mucking out stable yards in return for what little food they could spare. It wasn't enough to feed my mother and me, so I gave most of it to her. I gradually got weaker and weaker. I didn't starve to death though. Where I worked there was a mean horse who used to try to kick me. He had previously been abused, so he didn't like people. I was always very careful and didn't go near him, but this one day I was so weak and disoriented and didn't see that he was in the yard where I was cleaning. I was bending over, shovelling manure, when I heard a thud of hooves, then a rush of air. That was it. Next thing I was in Opaitu with Levi looking over me. It was surreal, to say the very least.

"I'm surprised I made it there as I hadn't been anything like an angel in my previous lives. Two of those had been lived as a Viking, where I stole and killed, and was pretty evil. Lucky for the world, I didn't live to a great age in either of those lives. However, in each subsequent life I progressed, until I finally managed to ascend into the next dimension. Opaitu is incredible, and full of scope for you to continue to grow and develop as an individual. You are the only ones to have ever been given the opportunity to see our world without earning your ascension in the usual way. You can't miss that opportunity.

"As for Levi and Gwen, they have come from a higher dimension. They are essentially light-beings and can move anywhere in less than a blink of an eye. They can transcend from one dimension to another – there is no limitation – because they no longer have physical bodies as we do. I guess one could think of them as gods, though they are actually part of a large force of goodness. In the Opaitu solar system they are our guardians, hence the fact that we call them Tuerians, from the Latin word *tueri*, which means 'protect'.

"We don't know much about them, only that we have the ability to ascend many levels until we reach their dimension. They protect us by keeping dark forces from entering our solar system, as well as being our mentors.

There is so much to show you. I can't even begin to tell you about the journey I have had over the last seven-hundred years. And I am still there, trying to ascend again. Or maybe not. I think I like it so much that I'm not really in any rush to move on. The choice is always ours.

"Getting back to you, Robyn, and the opportunity you have – this is unbelievable. It is astounding that the Universe is stepping in to help. Albeit indirectly. It was never expected to have to assist, as Earth has been given every opportunity to progress. It is unknown why the darkness is not lifting; in fact, it has got worse, and the end of Earth is in sight – sooner that you would think. I don't know for sure, but my assumption is that somehow dark forces from the galaxy we know as Zoltonia could be at work here. Perhaps they have managed to infiltrate Earth's space and time. I've tried to get Levi to confirm this, but he won't discuss it. I am not entitled to know. So, Earth and all life on Earth depends on you and the other youngsters. It's your destiny, Robyn. Don't fight it."

Robyn's eyes hadn't left Max's during his entire speech. She felt as though she was in a trance, spellbound to his every word. He was still holding her hands and staring intently into her eyes. She couldn't break the connection. Her mind raced as she felt herself capitulate. How could she deny Earth whatever help she was able to give? Even if it was a morsel of hope, she had to be prepared to give that. She nodded and in a dreamy voice she said, "Even though I feel like you have somehow drugged me with your words and touch, Max, I now know that I cannot turn away from this mission. That doesn't mean that I'm not scared, or don't feel inadequate; I am absolutely terrified. But I will do everything in my power to help."

Max leapt up and lifted Robyn above his head as though she was a feather. He laughed in delight as he swung her around, nearly hitting Ryan in the head with her feet as he did so. She laughed with him, as Rika and Ryan joined in. It was as though the room had been lit up with sunshine and rainbows. As Max put Robyn gently back on her feet, she understood where the rainbows where coming from; Max was flashing lights from his eyes again.

Ryan leapt up and hugged Robyn. "Robyn, I'm so happy you are going to be with me. It will be such an experience."

Max winked at Rika as he put his arm around her shoulder and gave her a huge grin.

Robyn slumped back onto the seat. "What have I done?" she whispered. Her head spun as she felt the now familiar reeling sensation rock her body. Her last thought, before blackness closed in, was that her life had changed forever.

The Universe is calling...

...will Earth respond?

ABOUT THE AUTHOR

Anne Cowell was born and raised in Zimbabwe, then moved to South Africa with her husband shortly after they were married. In 2002, with their two children, the family emigrated to New Zealand. Anne now lives on Auckland's North Shore with her family and much loved dog.

With a particular passion for dogs and horses, and an abiding love of nature, Anne began her writing career with children's picture books about animals, which she both wrote and illustrated. She now juggles her time between freelance accounting work, her writing, illustrating, and painting animal portraits.

www.annecowell.com